NO ORDER

Inspired by True Events

Elizabeth McCormick

No Order: Inspired by True Events
Elizabeth McCormick
Published March 2026
Little Creek Books
Imprint of Jan-Carol Publishing, Inc.

Cover Design: Provided by Elizabeth McCormick

ISBN: 978-1-970471-15-1
Library of Congress Control Number: 2026935524

You may contact the publisher:
Jan-Carol Publishing, Inc.
PO Box 701
Johnson City, TN 37605
publisher@jancarolpublishing.com
www.jancarolpublishing.com

All nurses everywhere, you are my unsung heroes.

I salute you!

Praise for

NO ORDER

"The experiences of this author on her road to a calling as a nurse health caregiver were a page turner. Let's hope all nurses have the same goal toward helping patients! I enjoyed her travel to the RN degree and experiences along the way very much."

— ★★★★★ AMAZON REVIEW

"I liked this book very much. In the medical field, it's hard to make others see a drastic mistake made by your superiors. This nurse was able to do that and more. She did put patients above herself! Good story."

— ★★★★★ AMAZON REVIEW

"I loved this story and found it true and shocking what this nurse had to go through."

— ★★★★★ AMAZON REVIEW

CHAPTER 1

"Save one person, you're a hero. Save a hundred, you're a nurse."
– UNKNOWN

It was a Monday morning. I barely made it out of the apartment on time for work. I'm diligent about my schedule, but as a single mom, there's always the hitch of making sure my kids are on time as well. My son, Willy, was my youngest and a senior in high school. Anne, my daughter, was at university and still came home for a warm meal and to do her laundry.

My Chevy kept up with traffic as I drove down the 417 into the heart of Ottawa. The calendar said it was March, but it was far from springtime. A tremendous snowstorm dumped a heavy white blanket, and I had to keep my windshield wipers on high. I said a little prayer on the highway, knowing full well what could happen in the event of an untimely accident.

Accidents were my main source of livelihood as an insurance claims adjuster. For over 20 years, I had been on the receiving end of phone calls from claimants who had experienced pain and suffering caused by automobile accidents. My job involved interviewing claimants to investigate these claims thoroughly to substantiate there wasn't any kind of fraud. Unfortunately, in my many years, the fraudulent claims seemed to outnumber the honest ones.

As I waited on the off-ramp leading to my office building, my mind wandered. A feeling of restlessness robbed me of sleep and ambition. After 40 years on this planet, I was beginning to doubt whether I wanted to remain in this dreary frozen tundra, for at least half the year, and whether the insurance job brought me any satisfaction. I would love to find a new opportunity in a warmer climate. But what and where?

The office was at its normal low hum. I found my desk was still covered by a mound of files left from the week before. Gabriella, my sweet friend and co-worker, who enjoyed one too many trips to Tim Hortons reflected by her thick waistline, poked her head up to greet me. She also handed me a sheet of paper.

"Good morning, Julie. Here's the list of your interview appointments."

"Thanks," I answered. "Happy Monday! Here we go."

I took a seat at my desk just as our supervisor, more like our commandant, Mrs. Murphy, came around. She was always poised with her hands clasped behind her back and walked the rows of desks to peer in on her subordinates. She was a permanent fixture ensuring the task at hand was done and done well. Mrs. Murphy, in her sensible shoes and tightly permed hair, had trained me all those years ago. She was a tough cookie on the outside, but inside, she had a softer core.

"A bee makes more honey when focused," Mrs. Murphy quipped as she walked past Gabriella and me. "Less fluttery and more inquiry!"

"Yes, ma'am," we replied.

Then it was nose-down while I worked the files of 80 outstanding cases. It was such an overwhelming workload to maintain. The clock was ticking with every single one of these claims. They needed to be closed out while new ones were opened. It was the kind of job with an endless cycle that you could do 24 hours a day, seven days a week, and never feel caught up.

One of my assigned calls was to a middle-aged couple who had been injured in a car accident. These new claimants had received severe injuries. I made an appointment to come out and see them. With the longevity of my career at the insurance company, I had earned the role of "road adjuster" and spent the majority of my days traveling to interview claimants. The company supplied me with a laptop, company car, and gas card.

A couple of weeks ago, Mrs. Murphy introduced us to our new claims manager, Toni. She seemed friendly yet tightlipped at the initial meet-and-greet with our team. Little did I know that things were about to take a harrowing turn.

With the keys to the company car in hand, I grabbed my briefcase containing my laptop and files and made a quick stop by Gabriella's desk. I glanced around and kept my voice low to avoid any reprimand from the lurking Mrs. Murphy.

"Hey," I whispered. "I appreciate your help. Let's get together for a movie night soon."

"I'll call ya," she whispered back. "Be careful on those snowy roads out there."

I nodded and headed for the main exit.

As I approached the doorway, Toni popped out of her office, and I noticed she watched me leave. Did she need something from me? I wondered. Since Toni said nothing, I shrugged and proceeded on my way.

During my drive to the suburbs of Ottawa, I pulled over for a brief trip to a grocery store to grab a few items. I had plenty of time before the appointment, and I needed ingredients to prepare tonight's dinner with my kids. When I returned to the company car, I noticed a blue four-door sedan parked a couple of spots down. There was a dark-haired man sitting behind the wheel.

As I continued on to my appointment, that blue sedan came into my rear-view mirror. *Peculiar*, I thought. Then the sedan disappeared. I arrived at an apartment complex for my scheduled interview with the claimants. Mr. and Mrs. G told me their version of the car crash that happened outside their church. They had been struck just as they were leaving worship service. An elderly man hit the gas pedal instead of the brakes, and his car flew from the parking lot and pinned them both beneath the vehicle right outside the church entrance. They both suffered concussions and hyperextension injuries, commonly known as whiplash. Mrs. G had a broken leg. Mr. G had a broken arm, and they both had rib fractures. Their injuries were supported by physicians' medical reports.

The couple required surgeries and treatments from occupational therapists, physical therapy, chiropractic, and massage. They also required payment for loss of income while they were in recovery and off of work. I took thorough notes on my laptop during the interview, gave them my business card, and informed them of how the process would unfold from this point forward. I could see the sincere concern on their faces. I could also tell by their meager furnishings that this couple probably lived paycheque to paycheque with a very little to non-existent savings account. My stomach had the familiar butterflies as I bid them goodbye. I knew their case needed prompt handling, which would require long hours to bring them the closure and financial support they so desperately desired. Thankfully, they had not retained a dark-sided lawyer who would have fueled the claim with fraud. My next step would be to go back to the office and follow up with their healthcare providers to collaborate on the severity of their injuries in order to push their case into the "priority" stack.

As I walked to the company car, I glanced over my shoulder and suddenly froze. That same blue sedan was parked in the apartment parking lot. The dark-haired man and I made eye contact. Instead of fear, I was immensely infuriated. Gabriella had shared some office gossip with me. Since Toni had arrived, some road adjusters reported instances of being followed while on their way to assignments. I thought it was just office chatter, but here I was, falling victim to it as well. As I marched toward the blue sedan, the man fired up the engine, floored it, and the car peeled out.

I had to pause for a moment as I sat behind the wheel of the company car. I was a little shaken. This entire scenario seemed strange to me. I had been working for the company for so long, and nothing like this had ever happened.

When I returned to the office, I was confronted by Toni.

She saw that I entered the office and yelled at me.

"Where were you?" she demanded.

"I had a scheduled interview," I replied. Her outburst caught me off guard. I opened my briefcase and showed her the interview forms I had completed from my meeting with Mr. and Mrs. G. She snatched them out of my hand and stormed back into her office. My colleagues all watched this encounter and then quickly cowered back to their desks.

Aside from the odd outburst from Toni, the rest of my day went as usual. I reviewed additional claims I had received for soft tissue injuries to the neck and back. I got caught up on emails and decided I would take my laptop and some files home to work on that night. I really wanted to focus on Mr. and Mrs. G's claim. It was my job to investigate medical assessments submitted by physicians, chiropractors, and occupational therapists. A lot of long hours and hard work were spent on each one of my pending cases.

As Gabriella and I prepared to leave for the night, another road adjuster, Larry, came up to us.

"Did you feel like you were being followed today?" he asked.

"As a matter of fact, a blue—"

"Four-door sedan," Larry finished my sentence.

"Yes! You too?"

"Uh-huh, I was followed three days last week. A dark-haired guy. I stopped to check on a sound system I had installed for a friend. I do that on the side for a little extra income—got twins, you know." Everybody in the office knew about Larry's twin boys. There were snapshots of his kids on almost every inch of his desk.

"I got reported, and now Toni wants to put me on probation. Watch your back!" warned Larry.

"Thanks for the heads up," I told him.

Larry gave Gabriella and me a friendly salute and left the office. Gabriella grabbed her coat and headed for the elevator. I always took the stairs. Gabriella had a pair of temperamental knees that were especially painful during the cold weather months.

"Aren't you coming?" she asked.

"You go on ahead. I need to check on something. If the guy is following road adjusters, it sounds more like surveillance to me."

"But we have employees who do surveillance on claimants, the ones we've found who report fraud. Why would the company put surveillance on their own employees? How creepy is that?"

"Very creepy!" I could feel my face redden with my response.

Later that evening, my laptop and files crowded the small dining table in my apartment. Willy found a free space and landed his notebook and textbook to do his homework. While I was cooking a turkey casserole, the phone rang, and I answered.

"Hello."

"Hey, Julie." It was my little sister, Jenny. She always knew I'd pick up the call if she rang around dinnertime.

"What's new?" I asked.

"Nothing exciting happening here in Kingston. Just came across an old family photo album. Gosh, Mom really loved springtime, didn't she? Remember all those bright yellow daffodils she'd plant around the house?"

"And she'd never let us pick them! What's the point of a flower garden if you can't pick the flowers!"

"For the benefit of the neighbors, I suppose," Jenny added.

"You're probably right," I agreed.

Jenny fell quiet. I knew by the silence on the other end of the line that she was missing Mom. The anniversary of our mother's death always made us melancholy around this time of the year. I was 26 when she died, and Jenny was 21. Losing our mother was a huge loss in both of our lives.

Willy lumbered into the narrow kitchen and tried to peek at the casserole in the oven. I hip-checked him away from the stove and swiped the Gameboy out of his grasp. He frowned and returned to his homework.

"You sound tired," Jenny broke her silence.

"When am I not exhausted?!" I exclaimed.

"NEVER!" Willy surprised me with his roaring response. I gave him a snide, side-eyed glance for eavesdropping. He kept his head down and scribbled with his pencil. I could never stay mad at my lanky and shaggy-haired son.

"Have you thought any more about a nursing career?"

Silence fell on my end of the line this time. I paced between the oven and the sink, then finally answered.

"I enjoy my job." I hadn't lied to my sister. It was the truth. I did enjoy the challenges each claim presented.

"Mom always thought you'd make a good nurse," Jenny muttered.

"Mom was a cheerleader for us both. I better go finish up dinner. Love you, Sis. Bye."

"Love you too." Jenny hung up.

I spun around and quietly watched Willy as he toiled away on his studies. When I was 18, I finished high school and applied for nursing school. The mandatory courses included two science and math. I was told to bring up my grades in chemistry. I didn't excel in chemistry or math, which made me change directions. By the age of 19, I went to Trent University and, three years later, completed a degree in history. That's also where I met my husband, Luke. During my time at Trent, I worked as a campus tour guide, and during the summer months, I continued part-time as a claims adjuster. The insurance company paid well, provided flexibility, and when my kids were born, I was able to work from home. It had been over a decade since Luke and I divorced. My job in insurance remained. But lately, the wanting of a career in nursing reawakened inside me.

CHAPTER 2

"Be nice to me...I may be your nurse someday, and remember, catheters and needles come in sizes that I choose!"

– UNKNOWN

The following week, I arrived at the office and could immediately tell that something was off. Instead of the usual subdued atmosphere, there was edginess and disruption. I noticed that there was a small group of executives blocking the doorway of Toni's office. As I passed by, I took a glimpse and noticed that Toni's desk was cleared, and her office seemed to be vacated.

When I sat down at my desk, Gabrielle quickly shuffled over to me.

"What's going on?" I asked in my normal hushed tone.

"Toni's been fired. She was ushered out by security a few minutes ago." Gabriella's mouth curled into a slight smile.

"Wow!" I sat up higher in my chair and peeked again in the direction of Toni's office. "She didn't last long."

"Apparently, she was using company funds inappropriately," Gabriella continued.

"Such as not-so-secret surveillance on her own employees!" I was shocked and couldn't contain my rage.

"You got it." Gabriella placed a calming hand on my shoulder.

"Ahem!" Mrs. Murphy interrupted the conversation. "Leadership will be recruiting a new claims manager. I'm sure the two of you have better things to do than spread office gossip."

"Yes, ma'am," Gabriella and I answered in unison.

It was time to return to my never-ending list of claimant calls. After almost two decades of service at the insurance company, I was promoted from claims adjuster to senior accident benefits adjuster. Over the last four years as a benefits adjuster, the philosophy of "guilty until proven innocent" came into play, mainly because 90% of the claims filed were fraudulent. Claimants were coached by what we liked to refer to as "darkside lawyers." They were the underbelly litigators and ambulance chasers in the legal field. These darkside lawyers would convince their clients (our claimants) that they were entitled to large sums of money based on little to zero evidence of personal injury. These darkside lawyers would also serve on defendants' cases and try to turn the tables with an unsubstantiated countersuit, which was more like a counterfeit suit!

As a senior accident benefits adjuster, my work delved into the investigation of cases. I left no stone unturned. I would analyze on-scene accident reports and medical reports, and review surveillance of the claimant in question. I would also inquire with third-party practitioners for medical examinations of the claimants if I got a feeling in my gut that their primary doctor didn't provide a thorough examination or diagnosis. The summation of my investigation would be passed along to the insurance company's legal team, who would use it as evidence when claimants went to trial. In 90% of these cases, the jury would return a verdict in favor of the claimant. The jurors would believe the medical reports of the darkside lawyer and the "darkside doctors." Many times, our surveillance would show the claimant being active with no sign of physical inabilities. The darkside lawyer would argue that the client happened to have a "good day" when they were recorded under surveillance. Judgments would be rendered in favor of the plaintiff (claimant) and a No Order of Acquittal would be obtained by the insurance company. The truth would lose, and the fraudulent lie would prevail.

This experience of reading medical reports and interviewing claimants (some of whom were legitimate patients under the care of therapists, doctors, and surgeons) prompted me to have a greater interest in the healthcare field. A career in nursing lingered just beyond my peripheral vision. Studying anatomy, internal functions of the body, and motor skill associations based on reports from occupational therapists and physical therapists intrigued me.

One of the claimants on my call roster was a nurse who was a few years older than me. Ms. V worked for a major hospital in Ottawa. The employee parking lot was located across a six-lane boulevard from the hospital. She had crossed that same intersection hundreds of times over the course of her employment. On one fateful morning, the nurse was walking in the designated crosswalk when a female teenage driver ran a red light and hit her, causing severe injuries. In Ms. V's case, this accident was life-altering. She had sustained a crushed pelvis and broken femur (hip) plus traumatic brain injury (TBI). After the teen's car hit her body, the nurse was flung into the windshield, and her head took the brunt of the impact. She would never fully regain her balance on two feet. She could not walk without the assistance of a cane or walker, and her TBI left her with impaired vision, diminished concentration, and memory issues. Even after her multiple surgeries and many months of therapy treatments, Ms. V was unable to return to a job that she loved and lived for. During my check-in calls with Ms. V, almost every conversation she shared with me wasn't so much about herself as it was about the triumphs and tribulations she had with her own patients. She told me that for her, "Nursing wasn't just a job; it was a calling."

The sad irony was that Ms. V was a "frequent flyer" patient at the very same hospital where she had once happily walked the halls as an employee. Due to her injuries, she was unable to return to work and landed on long-term disability. The process of returning claimants to wellness was extremely involved, given that a lot of the claims would take over two years. Ms. V was one of those types of claims. Notably, the two-year mark would significantly inhibit the possibility of the insured returning to work. Statistically, after injury, if a person has not resumed work, the likelihood of them doing so is negligible.

During the handling of Ms. V's claim, rehab was involved to return her to health as quickly as possible, along with many medical professionals, including physical therapists, chiropractors, neurologists, occupational therapists, and speech pathologists. Independent medical reports were documented and possible job studies were done by a career coach to determine her transferable skills. Each time, the chance of Ms. V returning to her nursing career, or any occupation, diminished. And that broke both of our hearts. All she looked forward to was being able to return to her previous occupation.

I made sure Ms. V's treatment plans were approved, time off from work was substantiated, and that her employer completed documentation confirming her employment and income earned. Dealing with the insured teenage driver, her parents, and their lawyers in an effort to return Ms. V to a productive life was the most challenging. The challenge was what I enjoyed most. It gave me tremendous job satisfaction if I was able to get the claimant back to work and/or as close to pre-accident health as possible.

The parents of the teenage driver at fault had hired a darkside lawyer who argued that the teen had not run a redlight, and it was Ms. V who was at fault for stepping into a crosswalk at the wrong time. Despite many eye-witness accounts that were reported at the accident scene vindicating Ms. V, this darkside lawyer had dragged on the case, which created unjust emotional and physical agony for my claimant. These darkside lawyers knew that the longer the claim remained open, the greater chance they had for the insurance company to settle the case. On the flip side, the longer a claim remained open, the greater the chance for a higher monetary settlement for the injured party.

The insurance company and I had been representing and fighting for Ms. V for close to three years. I was determined to get justice and accommodation for Ms. V. I dialed the familiar number, and she answered.

"Hello." Her voice was wispy and tired.

"Hello, V," I replied.

"Julie, my dear! How are you?" A brightness from her arose, and it made me smile to be called "dear." I couldn't recall the last time anyone had used that word and my name in the same sentence.

"I'm well. Tell me how you're doing?"

"There's good days and bad. Wish my hip would heal properly, still have a lot of pain just getting out of bed every morning. And there's the persistent headaches."

"Let's get you signed up for a neurologist for the headaches and more PT to help with that hip," I suggested.

"The clinic told me that I don't qualify for any continued PT," Ms. V replied.

That did not sound correct to me. Ms. V proceeded to tell me that the treatment center called saying that they had not received any recent payments for her treatment, and we were looking for reimbursement. The clinic warned Ms. V that she may be sent to collections. The brightness in Ms. V's voice was quickly replaced by fear. I immediately ordered her file from storage, and my next priority was to follow up with the teenager's insurance company and get the treatment center accounts receivable off Ms. V's back.

"Let me look into this for you," I reassured Ms. V.

"You have such a good demeanor of care. You'd probably make a good nurse someday!"

"Funny you should say that!" Her comment surprised and thrilled me. I figured she was the perfect person to pose the next question to. "What does it take to be a good nurse?"

"A lot of hard work and dedication...and a really good pair of shoes!" she laughed. "Seriously, though, it also takes a lot of sacrifice. You always...and I do mean *always*...need to put the needs of your patients ahead of your own. Being a nurse puts you on the front line between life and death sometimes. But when you do help someone feel better, there's nothing else like it, a euphoria that can't be matched. You can really help change a life for the better."

It was during this poignant conversation that I thought, *Okay, I'm going to register for the RN course. This was a sign that I should do so.*

"I'll get a continued order for your physical therapy. Don't worry about those reimbursement calls from the treatment center. I'll get that covered as well. Shall I arrange transportation for you to get to your appointments?"

"Well…I don't recall anyone calling me from the PT clinic." That was her TBI talking. Her short-term memory loss was evident. Just as fast as she spoke about something, poof! It vanished as if through a sieve.

An email popped up on my screen from the file assistant in storage. Ms. V's full case file would arrive in a matter of minutes. I had to clear my calendar for the rest of the morning to get Ms. V squared away. I also had an email up on my screen that proved her PT had been extended, and I quickly forwarded that to the receptionist at the treatment clinic as a letter of confirmation. As for Ms. V's outstanding treatment bill, that was expedited to the teenage driver's insurance company with a warning about "failure to comply." Being a senior benefits adjuster brought out authoritative gusto in me, and I wasn't afraid to use it.

Aside from the "guilty until proven innocent" mentality, there's upholding the oath of insurance, which is "to place our insureds back into their previous financial position prior to suffering their loss." I was driven to give my full dedication to Ms. V—a good, honest, and hard-working woman, who was a victim that truly deserved to be made whole.

"I'll be in touch soon. Get some rest and take care, Ms. V."

"Thank you for calling, Julie. You take care too."

Over the next several hours, I scoured over Ms. V's file. Once I was done, she was registered for more therapeutic appointments and never received another call from the treatment center regarding payments.

After reviewing and re-reading all of the medical reports and treatment plans, my brain felt like it was on fire. Gabriella must have noticed, as she brought me a refreshing glass of ice water.

"All's well with Ms. V's case," I told her as I heaved a heavy sigh.

"You're such a sleuth when it comes to the investigation stuff," Gabriella said.

"Yeah, well, it comes from the many years of experience and tons of digging for the facts."

I took a long drink. My 40 years were almost a blur when I turned back to my monitor screen. "You ever get the feeling you were meant to do something else?" I asked Gabriella.

She shook her head. "Yeah, but what?"

"I think I want to be a nurse. Go back to school, nursing school. Am I nuts?"

"No! Absolutely not. I think you'd make a great nurse! What about me, do you think I could join you at nursing school?" She leaned enthusiastically over my desk.

"You'd have to ante up for a pair of really good orthopedic shoes," I answered as my eyes floated down past Gabriella's face to her pudgy knees. Her eyes went there too.

"Maybe a desk job is best after all," she pouted. "Are you going to do it? Really study to be an RN?"

"To quote the great Elvis Presley, 'It's now or never!'" Gabriella and I shared a hearty chuckle, and soon Mrs. Murphy sidled up to my desk.

"Care to share what's going on here?" she commanded.

"Would it be possible for me to take a leave of absence to take a registered nursing course?"

"What do I look like? A miracle worker? You'll have to take that up with HR. Nursing? Hmmm. Aren't you past your prime for being a medical student?"

And thus began the naysayer's campaign toward my goal of becoming a nurse. I wasn't about to let Mrs. Murphy or anyone else with her same frame of mind stop me. I was determined to go back to nursing school. I spoke with human resources, and upon any acceptance into a nursing program, I could be granted part-time employment status with the insurance company. They could keep my benefits package intact due to my longevity with the company. That was a true blessing!

Later that evening, I spoke with Willy and Anne and told them about my endeavor. Willy was wide-eyed, and I could tell by the way he looked me straight in the face that he couldn't imagine his mom starting a different career path.

"Mom, don't you want to retire?" This Gen Zer had no idea that retirement was at least another 20 years away. He almost looked hurt and angry when I laughed at his response.

The other news for my kids was that we would be moving from the main apartment to the basement apartment in our house, which I owned. It was smaller, more affordable, and easier to manage. Funds would be tight since I would be working less, and I still needed to keep a roof over our heads. The main upstairs apartment where we lived now would be rented out for extra income. Willy wasn't thrilled about that, but he understood. Anne was on board with my new plan just as long as she could still drop by for a hot meal or free groceries. I'll admit it was weird to acknowledge that my daughter and I would be in school at the same time. Anne knew I was a go-getter, and I could tell by her grin that she was in full support of my decision.

As I scanned the website of the registered nurse program, I wrote down all of the necessary materials that would be required for submitting an application. A high school transcript? A university degree transcript made sense. Contacting Trent University would be no problem, but to go all the way back to Bayside High, gosh! That was over 23 years ago!

The next morning, I woke up with a fresh perspective and I was undeterred. I called my old high school and spoke to a very nice yet what sounded to be an ancient secretary. She took my information, maiden name, and my parents' home address, and after a few hours, she called me back. She had gone into the archives and located my transcript.

"I'll pop these in the mail, and you should receive them in a couple of days," she said.

"Fine! That's terrific! Thank you," I replied.

I managed that hurdle—I thought. But I hit a snag when the actual transcript arrived. I noticed that there was a mark for physics on my high school transcript. I had never taken physics, but I recalled my sister had; it was her mark that appeared on my transcript. *No use in asking for a correction*, I thought to myself. I decided to use it, relieved that I wouldn't have to bring up my chemistry mark for the nursing school application.

When I crawled into bed, I lay there in deep thought. The past 20 years played like a movie up on the blank ceiling. Finishing 13th grade, applying to nursing school, being denied, getting the claims adjuster job at the insurance company, getting accepted into Trent University, meeting Luke, dating Luke, making future plans with Luke, graduating from university, obtaining my degree, getting married, going back to the insurance company, having my babies, feeling lost in my marriage, wrangling not two but three kids because Luke was as reckless as a child, the divorce, being promoted to senior benefits adjuster, working, working, working, being a mom throughout to my precious kids, and—now—finding peace and solace, hoping and praying that this second time around I can follow my dream of becoming a nurse. All the while, I shoved back the little nagging voice in my head which constantly reminded me that I was a 40-something about to enter the race of a 20-something.

CHAPTER 3

"Knowing is better than wondering, waking is better than sleeping, and even the biggest failure–even the worst–beats the hell out of never trying."

– Grey's Anatomy

Ten weeks had gone by since I had submitted my application to Nursing School. I awoke each morning with a pit in my stomach. The financial situation of returning to school made me very hesitant about becoming a full-time student.

After weeks of contemplation, I decided to plan out steps toward becoming an RN. First, I looked into a personal support worker (PSW) program. The classes were in the evenings and the schedule was manageable for me after working full-time at my insurance day job.

Attending the PSW course got me into the right frame of mind for being a student again. The homework was relatively easy to comprehend, and the program targeted hands-on work right away. Upon graduating from the PSW program, I found an evening and weekend position at a long-term care facility for residents with cerebral palsy (CP). Tonight was to be my first shift at New Horizons House.

But first, I had to deal with a rather large case involving six claimants. The case involved one driver and five passengers in a van that were stuck from behind while en route for an early morning mushroom-picking excursion. This group claimed that they all sustained neck and back injuries as a result of the rear-end impact. After interviewing all of the claimants, I became acutely aware that the incident may not have unfolded as they reported. This entire case was beginning to reek of fraud.

When I interviewed each of the six, they told me, "I went forward," upon impact from the rear-end collision. With neck and back injuries, you're dealing with soft tissue and hyperextension injuries. To be a victim of whiplash, the neck whips backward first, then snaps forward. It's almost physically impossible to lunge forward when hit from behind. Think of standing, then someone comes up behind you and kicks you in the rear. Will you fall forward first? No, chances are greater that you'll fall backward, like having your feet kicked out from under you.

How they received their neck and back injuries came into question. Our new claims manager, Howard, had delegated this case to me. He had taken the time to have one-on-one meetings with each of his claims adjusters when he took on his position. He seemed like a decent guy who earnestly had employees' backs when it came to disproving fraudulent cases. Due to my seniority and longevity with the company, Howard knew I would give due diligence and dig through all the muck to determine if the people in the van had actual injuries worthy of payment and restitution. I was tasked with whether or not these six people were going to receive a "yes" or "no" when it came to proving they were hurt in the accident.

The initial medical reports from their physicians came back with a diagnosis of hyperextension injuries for all six. However, upon individual interviews, their accounts of the accident varied each time they were asked. They each claimed the rear-end impact affected their physical capacities in different ways. Their inability to tell the same story more than once threw up a massive red flag in my investigation. With the support of Howard, I sent requests that all six go through independent medical examinations.

Meanwhile, I followed up on the case of Mr. and Mrs. G who had been hit by a car at the entrance to their church. Both of them had qualified for continued rehabilitation benefits and physical therapy. They both were to be placed on short-term disability to gain income during their recovery times. I was upholding the principle of insurance "to place the insured back into the health and financial situation they were positioned in or as close as possible prior to suffering the loss." After further investigation, it was discovered that the elderly driver who accidently hit Mr. and Mrs. G had taken prescribed medication which impaired his ability to operate a motorized vehicle. He drove despite the precautions indicated on the prescription bottle label and warning by his prescribing physician. He was found 100% at fault, and his insurance company would be covering any and all present-day and long-term care needs for Mr. and Mrs. G. There was a high probability that Mr. and Mrs. G may plateau in their rehabilitation, and complete recovery from their injuries may never be achieved.

At the end of the Friday workday, I went into the ladies' restroom to check my tote bag for my scrubs and my pair of leather Dansko shoes. When I emerged, I caught a smirk on Mrs. Murphy's face. Somewhere beneath her wrinkles was a woman who probably envied my shot at a new career beginning. I accompanied Gabriella to the elevator.

"Those look like really comfortable shoes," Gabriella commented.

I did a goofy pose like I was on a fashion shoot. My antics made Gabriella giggle. She had an infectious laugh and soon we were both giggling when the elevator door opened. As we stepped inside, I waved happily to Mrs. Murphy, and to my utter amazement, she nodded, and I think I actually caught her smiling. The elevator doors closed. As we descended, nervous butterflies flitted in my belly. Gabriella sensed it.

"Got the jitters about starting your shift at New Horizons?"

"It's all part of the training process."

"Good for you for putting yourself through the process," Gabriella said and gave me a gentle elbow jab. We exchanged grins, and the elevator doors opened.

* * *

I parked on the street beside the cluster of houses that had been converted into the New Horizons complex. From the outside, it looked like any regular group of homes. Inside was a different story. I pulled my hair up into a ponytail as I walked through the front door of house number three. Each of these buildings (homes) housed up to four to five CP (cerebral palsy) long-term care residents. This facility ran more like a group home than a healthcare institution. The evening/overnight shifts had a skeleton crew on staff. I was warned about this when I accepted the position. The only other person on staff with me was Kelly. She had been with the New Horizons group for seven years and moved up the ladder to manager. She was lean and had a mop of hair that was always bound up in a messy blonde bun. Many of the residents were wheelchair-bound because of their CP.

My duty as a PSW was to make sure the residents' needs were being met. This involved toileting, bathing, feeding, administering therapies, and ensuring their mental and physical care was addressed and documented. On occasion, PSW duties were called upon in more than one house during my shift. This was the kind of work that always had a revolving door when it came to staffing. I won't lie, it was hard and strenuous work. Physically, there was a lot involved with moving, positioning, and lifting a resident in and out of bed and in and out of their wheelchair, especially when it came to showering and bathing.

Working as a PSW meant that I had to double up on my lifting and hauling abilities. There was only one Hoyer lift that was shared between the five homes in the New Horizons complex. Kelly thought that was ridiculous, and so did I! A tight budget was to blame. Expecting staff to overexert themselves day after day (or night after night) surely resulted in workers' compensation cases and time off adding to the debacle of staff shortages and insufficient resident care. It didn't take long from the time I started working at New Horizons for me to gather enough evidence and documentation to serve the administration to warrant the purchase of a second and third Hoyer lift. Kelly didn't have the time or the expertise in this sort of paperwork, but I did. Kelly and the residents were so thankful when those new lifts arrived. I was proud that my plan got the attention of the administration. Maybe my years of experience and my age played to my advantage in being an advocate for the residents and staff. I was driven to bring the best care possible to the residents and save the backs of the staff.

My next step toward becoming an RN was to enroll in a registered practical nurse (RPN) program. I submitted my application and was accepted. The RPN studies were much more intense than the PSW course. The RPN was a one-year program, and the studies required my full-time attention. I left the PSW position at New Horizon to return to working part-time at the insurance company. I spent my days studying and attending the RPN classes. Burning the candle at both ends was frying my neurons but I pressed on. Back at the insurance office, I hunkered down with a huge mug of coffee and worked my way through files as Mrs. Murphy raised inquisitive eyebrows and hovered nearby.

Stressing over finances also hung over my head like a heavy cloud. I spoke with my sister, Jenny, and she agreed to lend me some money to cover living expenses. I knew completing the RPN would open many doors for me, and I promised to pay her back.

Meanwhile, Willy and Anne did their best to be self-sufficient. Having them pop in and out was a good distraction for me. Being their mom was a job that I cherished and could never ignore. We would sit together and watch a movie or a sports game, hockey most likely, in our downtime together. Occasionally, we also enjoyed our winter skate on the Rideau Canal. Downtown Ottawa was so pretty in the winter. Willy and Anne were outstanding skaters from playing years of hockey.

With the completion of the RPN license, I was immediately accepted into the RN program. Nursing school was now within my reach. It was crazy to think how much studying I had done over the last year and a half, and now I had three more years of reading and exams ahead to become a RN.

The first day of nursing school had arrived. I was easily one of the oldest, mature students in the entire class. The stack of textbooks each of us lugged around was like carrying a backpack filled with cement. There was so much material to read and learn. It was an overwhelming adjustment. It had been such a long time since I had been on campus and in "student" mode. The one thing that brought some sense of stability to this entire experience was my seasoned instructor, Doris. She was a pear-shaped maternal figure with a voice that carried and snapped you to attention. Doris handed out plenty of study guides and course readings. Teaching wasn't just an occupation for Doris; it was second nature, and her vast knowledge of nursing flowed out of her like a steady stream.

"If there's one thing you should take away from nursing school, it's this. Learn to have a therapeutic boundary and barrier. You'll want to get emotionally involved with your patients. Trust me, you should only be involved enough in order to provide excellent care and a good rapport. Be friendly and professional, always. The way you deal with your patients should be the same way you deal with your friend, child, or mother. But don't let yourself get attached; that's where the barrier needs to be." These words of wisdom from Doris struck a chord within me right at the start and were engraved in my memory.

One chart Doris introduced us to was called "Maslow's Hierarchy of Needs." I found this to be so interesting and true to a point. The chart is a psychology theory of an individual's motivation. The needs in each level of the triangle must be met before an individual moves onto the next level.

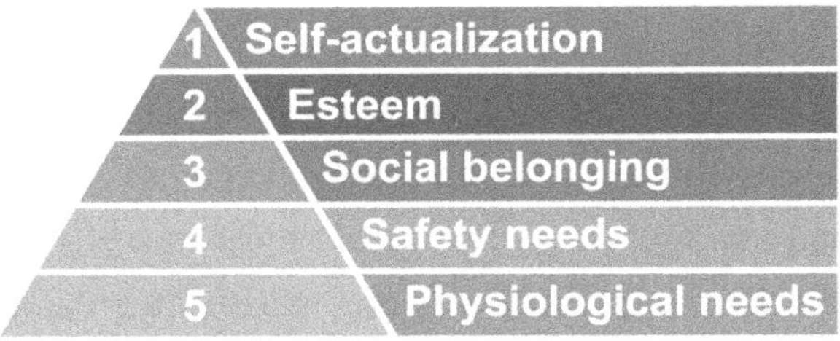

1 Self-actualization
2 Esteem
3 Social belonging
4 Safety needs
5 Physiological needs

By the end of that first week, Doris suggested we form study groups. Because several of my fellow students and I held jobs, Doris knew that a prime way to stay on top of the coursework was to connect with other RN students. A fiery red-headed 20-something named Amber and a foreign student from Italy, Philipo, became my study buddies. Philipo was an actual RN from Italy. He was in his early 30s and needed the courses to obtain his nursing registration in Canada.

My evenings at home warped into a study frenzy. The new routine required the apartment to be quiet, completely quiet, in order for me to focus. This drove Willy nuts, but he got a lot of use out of those stereo headphones I bought him. He was also exiled to his room if he wanted to watch TV or do any kind of gaming. The only sound I could tolerate when I studied was the hush of the night outside our window. The kitchen table was filled with notebooks, textbooks, and anatomy charts. I was exhausted yet diligent. Many times, it would be past 2 a.m. before I relished and crawled into bed.

In addition to the classes on campus, Doris required her students to have practicum experiences. A chance to put our class learning and theories to work as a quicker way to gain hands-on experience. Of course, I signed up right away. In doing so, Doris was able to assign me a preceptor, who I was able to shadow from at a senior long-term care facility.

A small group of students including me and our instructor, Doris, waited near the reception area of the senior facility. The atmosphere in the facility was welcoming; they tried to make the place feel less institutional and homier. The environment in this place was a far cry from New Horizons. Calm instrumental music playing overhead. The existing staff were escorting and wheeling residents to the dining area. Doris had given patient assignments. Before meeting our patients, we were allowed to review their charts and take notes of their diagnosis and medical history.

"Dinner time is a great opportunity to introduce yourself to the senior resident," Doris said.

My patient's chart read: *Owen. Age 78, severe stroke, nonverbal, paralyzed on the left side. Enjoys dogs and strawberry ice cream.*

The entourage of nursing students followed the staff and residents to the dining area. Our instructor met up with the facility's charge nurse. They both took this opportunity to observe our interaction with the residents. We were paired with a preceptor, and I was guided over to meet Owen. He was parked in his wheelchair at the end of a table he shared with one other male resident. I could tell that at one time he had been a man of tall stature and probably held an occupation of some importance. His hands were smooth, with no scars from calluses like that of a laborer. His idleness and curved posture didn't hinder the kind blue eyes that tracked me as I sat beside him.

"Hello there, Owen," I said. "My name's Julie. I'm here to visit and help you with dinner. Would that be all right with you?"

Owen's right eyebrow twitched. I took that as a sign for "yes." The server delivered trays of roast beef dinner, gravy with mashed potatoes, and a vegetable medley.

"If you finish all this, there's ice cream for dessert," the server winked.

"I hear strawberry ice cream is your favorite," I added.

Owen's head bobbed in agreement. I placed a napkin across his lap. He slowly raised his right arm, and his hand extended to grasp his fork. As he tried to jab at the sliced beef, the fork slid across his plate. I naturally assisted and helped his hand successfully stab morsels of beef. With great concentration, he raised his fork to his opened mouth, then chewed and swallowed. This process was repeated until his plate had been cleaned of every last bite of food.

I was the center of this one-sided dinner conversation with Owen. I told him about my entry into the nursing field after a long stay in insurance claims. Then I shared tidbits about Willy and Anne. For a time or two his eyes would pause on my face then return to his fork. After he placed down his fork for the last time, I dabbed at the gravy stuck in the corners of his mouth.

A cup containing scoops of strawberry ice cream arrived from the server. The corner of Owen's mouth curled into a lop-sided smile. His eyes looked to me and I couldn't help but smile too. I held the cup while Owen dug into the ice cream with his spoon, much like Willy did as a child when he'd scoop sand from a sandbox. This was a delightful moment I shared with Owen.

When Owen and the other residents had completed their dinners, the PSW staff and students returned residents to their rooms. I wheeled Owen to his studio suite at the end of the hall. The staff motioned for me to retrieve Owen's pajamas from a hook on the adjoining bathroom door. His name was printed on the inside collar and waistband. It reminded me of when I had to label my children's winter clothing when they went off to kindergarten. The worker also had me bring a fresh set of disposable underwear. The familiar "rip" of Velcro fasteners was heard as I assisted the staff member with Owen's change into his overnight garments. We practiced the appropriate and safest way to turn a patient in bed. With his paralysis, it was difficult for Owen to offer his assistance in this process. Any humility this older gentleman had was long gone, and in its place was a man who had succumbed to this diminished flame of life. Once he was dressed and comfortable, I patted his hand.

"It was nice to meet you, Owen. I look forward to visiting with you again."

That right eyebrow twitched, and his right hand shuffled across his body to clasp my hand. In his eyes, I thought I saw a sweet surrender. The staff member and I lowered the lights in his room as Owen laid propped up in his single bed.

Doris gathered us in a corner of the empty dining area to discuss our interactions. She gave pointers to the other students and mentioned the apprehension she observed. To me, she only said, "Keep up the good work." As we were leaving the facility, the preceptor that I had been paired with trotted up to the charge nurse. I saw them rush down the hall to Owen's room.

"What's going on?" I asked Doris.

She held out her arm to prevent me from following the staff. "Wait here."

I did as I was told and wrung my hands. A few moments later, the charge nurse had a quick and private conversation with my instructor. By this time, the other students had left. As Doris approached, I knew something was wrong.

"Mr. Owen has expired. It was nothing you did, Julie. It was his time."

My shoulders slumped. Is this all part of the process? It felt like someone was standing on my chest. My mind was spinning and frantically throwing up bricks for a therapeutic barrier. I left the building and wandered to my car. My assigned patient had died. Am I ready...really ready...to be a nurse and deal with this part of the process?

CHAPTER 4

"Bound by paperwork, short on hands, sleep, and energy, nurses are rarely short on caring."

– Sharon Hudacek

It was December 2003, and the holiday season was in full swing. I was in my final semester of nursing school. I had set the bar high and put a lot of pressure on myself. I completed the RPN (registered practical nurse) course first, which took a full year. That was the final opportunity in which the program was offered over a one-year timeframe. If I hadn't taken it that year, the program would have been changed to two and a half years. I couldn't set aside that long for schooling. I knew I had to bust my butt to take the course and pass it the first year. I didn't know what I was in for. There was so much to learn, tons of material crammed into one year that was later spread across two and a half years. It was a huge load on me and the other students. Twelve months of jam-packed, hard, and intense studies.

When I was accepted into the Canadian RN program, I knew that would be a three-year commitment. Thankfully, one semester's worth of credits was applied towards RN school from having completed the RPN course. So here I was, paying a mortgage, working part-time, borrowing money from my sister and the Canadian government. I also qualified for and received a $3,000 grant from the Canadian government. I studied in every free moment I had, even if it was for only five to ten minutes. There was so much to learn.

Aside from the pressure I put upon myself, there was also pressure from the RN program. They only permitted students to repeat a course once if they didn't pass it the first time. If they didn't pass on the second try, then the student was rejected from the program. Perfect attendance was also required. I wasn't allowed to miss any days of the course at all. All of the studying, attendance, and participation branded a deeper discipline into me and my routine. Being in my 40s, I thought I already had a pretty good grasp of discipline, but nursing school made me have precision on time management.

I was at the point where I almost felt as if nursing school was a form of academic torture. I had written pages and pages of notes that I studied over and over again. Over the past five semesters of nursing school, I kept thinking to myself, why am I doing this? I knew quitting wasn't an option and there was no looking back because I was so dissatisfied working in insurance. But keeping up this pace and regiment was so tremendously hard. I know it was difficult on my family too. I carved out time once a week to have pizza night with my kids. While I got updates on Willy and Anne's lives, I tried not to discuss my load from school.

When I studied, I couldn't handle any distractions at all. Other nursing students would talk about how they liked to play music in the background when they studied. Not me! I had to have silence so my mind could focus and pour all of my energy into the nursing material. I had to sit down in a quiet space where I could study and write notes. My day started at 0700, between going to classes and studying. It didn't end until around 2200. The only relaxation I found was cuddling with my cat, Chance. He would slink around my legs, letting me take a break and give him pets. What a sweet cat he was, and I loved him dearly. Willy and I found Chance on the road on a cold rainy night; he was emaciated and sickly. I nursed him back to health, so it was fitting that we named him "Chance." At times, I would be in a game of "get back" whenever Chance tried to pounce up onto the table. He would attempt to traipse over the stacks of textbooks and papers I had scattered on the dining table as I studied.

Understanding medical terminology was like learning a new language. There were terms like "diaphoretic." I had no clue to the meaning of that word before I started my nursing courses. There was a huge amount of knowledge to obtain. In order for me to learn, first I had to understand how something works. Once I understood the physiology of a bodily system, I could remember its function and build more learning upon it.

While I was in nursing school, I rarely saw anyone besides my kids. I didn't have time to socialize. The only people outside of my family circle were Amber and Philipo. Most of the time, we would meet at Amber's place. She was in a central location in Ottawa. We would study together on a Saturday or Sunday or on a day we had off from school and work. We usually spent around four to five hours together. During that time, we'd study for about three hours and share a meal. If there was a test coming up, we'd definitely get together to study.

An exam on the abdominal organs was scheduled before Christmas. Amber had copious notes about the liver, its functions and diseases. She'd written up an entire stack of flash cards. We quizzed each other and repeatedly went through the organs of the body, the functions, and the diseases until I was cross-eyed. The human body is very complicated. We discussed normal liver functions, then we'd switch to abnormal liver functions and how the abnormalities would lead to diseases of the liver. For instance, cirrhosis of the liver could be caused by drinking excessive amounts of alcohol, but it could also be caused by other factors unrelated to alcohol consumption.

Since Philipo had worked as an RN in Italy for five years, he provided insight and actual situations based on his background and experiences. As he shared patient stories with us, I was drawn in by his dark mocha eyes and his sultry Italian accent. I had to really concentrate on his actual words and not his enticing wet lips. There had been a time or two when I had given Philipo a ride back to his place after our study sessions. Each time, he gave me a friendly invitation to join him inside. I politely declined. The adventurous side of me was in a tug-o-war with the sensible side. I had to keep the relationship platonic or risk having my mind blown by a handsome Italian lover.

If I had been 10 years younger, I would have accepted his invitation in a milli-second. 42-year-old me had to keep her wits about her. What I was learning in my study group was far greater than anything I could have learned on my own. Exchanging our notes, thoughts, and experiences was so valuable to me. Nursing was a huge medical and scientific field that you had to be engulfed in in order to embrace it and educate yourself.

One of the hardest topics for me was obstetrics. It involved double duty, studying the bodily functions of the mother during pregnancy and the fetus's development during pregnancy in both normal and abnormal situations. There were so many complications that could possibly occur during pregnancy. Just studying it made me revisit my times as an expectant mother. I was glad I wasn't aware of all the things that could go wrong for a pregnant mother and baby. I almost felt sympathetic to the younger female students in my class who couldn't hide their faces of horror when we reviewed the content and watched a video of an actual birth.

Another topic that highly interested me was infectious diseases, how they spread, and the implications on patients. Our instructor, Doris, had our class read the case study about "Typhoid Mary." Mary Mallon was an Irish cook who worked for many wealthy families in the New York area from 1900 to 1907. She was an asymptomatic carrier of the bacteria linked to Typhoid fever. Mary did not believe she was a carrier and refused to be tested voluntarily. A doctor ordered her to be detained by the police, and through testing Mary was found to be a carrier and was placed into isolation. She never understood the implications of Typhoid and appealed the decision of her quarantine. She was released and returned to cooking for a hotel in New York City in 1915, which sparked another outbreak. The doctor who discovered Mary's condition was a female by the name of Dr. Sara Josephine Baker. Dr. Baker was an advocate for public health and hygiene and worked to bring this communicable disease under control.

As history would have it, Severe Acute Respiratory Syndrome (SARS) hit in the summer of 2003, and it delayed our nursing courses for one semester. The hospitals wouldn't allow students in until the SARS outbreak was under control.

The headline of *The Globe and Mail* on April 1, 2003, read "Ottawa steps up SARS battle," stating health officials in Ontario warned the outbreak could easily spread across the country. Every hospital was to abide by the screening and isolation protocols.

Speaking of outbreak, Doris had us watch the movie *Outbreak*, starring Dustin Hoffman and Rene Russo. It was a Hollywood depiction of what would happen if there was a lethal spread of a contagion. SARS, now referred to as coronavirus, was airborne and spread by droplets in saliva, much the same way as the common cold or flu. SARS had originated in China, and it had spread to over 30 countries and killed close to 800 victims. The World Health Organization (WHO) coordinated an international investigation with the assistance of the Global Outbreak Alert and Response Network (GOARN) and worked closely with health authorities in affected countries to provide epidemiological, clinical, and logistical support and to bring the outbreak under control.[1]

By the time Canada had created the SARS vaccine, three RNs had died, plus the doctor who invented the vaccine along with 44 Canadians. If the doctors and hospital administrations had given the isolation orders sooner, many deaths could have been prevented. The RNs on the front lines requested orders and instead they received resistance from hospital administrations. "No Order" was a common response. The refusals to administer isolations caused CoV-1, otherwise known as SARS, to spread widely.

A few hours had passed, and Amber collected back her flashcards. I gathered up my notebooks and textbooks and shoved them into my backpack. Philipo stood and stretched to loosen up his muscles from sitting so long. His stretching forced his sweater to hike up, and I got a glimpse of his bare six-pack belly. Whoa!

---

[1] History was going to repeat itself in a big way. The lessons learned in 2003 had long been forgotten when the COVID-19 outbreak took place in 2020.

"Shall we go out for coffee?" Philipo offered.

"I've got an assortment of teas and baked shortbread cookies," offered Amber.

"How about a homecooked Christmas dinner?" My offer turned both of their heads.

"Oh gosh!" exclaimed Amber.

"How lovely," responded Philipo.

"I would like to invite you both to join me and my family for Christmas Eve, if you don't already have plans."

"I'd love to come, but my family is expecting me," answered Amber.

"I can't afford a plane ticket home, so set a plate for me," Philipo replied with a smoldering smile.

"Will do! See you in class on Monday. I have a feeling we're going to ace this exam."

I grabbed a couple of Amber's shortbread cookies and headed to the door. I had to escape from Philipo, who hadn't yet had a chance to put his shoes on. I was out like a flash!

The following week, Amber, Philipo, and I passed the exam. A happy triumph for us as we completed the semester and dispersed for the holiday break.

Back at my apartment, I found Willy putting the finishing touches on our modest little Christmas tree. His girlfriend, Natalie, was with him. I noticed she had her arm wrapped around his waist. Hmm...young love. He had started dating this girl about the time I entered nursing school. As fate would have it, she was also in nursing school. We commiserated on assignments.

"I didn't know it was going to be this hard," Natalie remarked on more than one occasion. And I had to agree—it was hard!

Anne arrived just as I was unpacking groceries for our holiday feast. The kids' eyes bulged when I hoisted up the 15-pound organic turkey. I joked around like it was a trophy. The kids got a laugh out of it. My face beamed as I prepared all of the ingredients. I loved to cook. Every Christmas, I would make an enormous turkey. I used a 10cc syringe, filled it with melted butter, and injected it all around the bird. It turned out so juicy. Anne helped make my dressing from scratch and the mashed potatoes. I served roasted turnips too, which was a Canadian tradition. But the delicacy my family always looked forward to at Christmastime was my butter tarts. The creamed, brown sugar filling with pecans or raisins and a buttery crust was absolutely delicious.

Later on, guests arrived, and places were set at my table for Anne, Willy, Natalie, Jenny, and Philipo. I sat at the head of the table. Philipo did the honors of carving the turkey with the precision of a surgeon. We feasted until our bellies were full and the evening turned to night. After dessert, the kids left to check out the newest Christmas movie in the theater. Jenny had to be on her way to Kingston before the roads iced over. We loaded up her car with gifts and leftovers. As I waved goodbye to my sister, it left just Philipo and I. He held the door open for me as we went back inside. Then he presented me with a gift and insisted I open it. I unwrapped a narrow box and discovered a beautiful liquor bottle inside.

"It's Limoncello from Italy. Made from artisans in a neighboring village," he said proudly. Philipo poured the sunshine-yellow substance into two small glasses. We raised our glasses in a toast. "To following dreams," he grinned.

"Cheers!" I smiled.

Our glasses clinked and I took a slow and savory sip of the limoncello. The zesty lemon drink enlivened my insides and made me truly feel like I was tasting the warmth of the sun. Philipo and I sat on my sofa. It wasn't long before he poured us a refill. Outside the window, snow was gently falling. My eyes were drawn to the white flakes as they glided down.

"I don't think I will ever get used to snow. How do you stand it?" Philipo inquired.

"Actually, I've been thinking of moving to a warmer climate." My voice was mellow, and I was feeling quite relaxed. Drinking the limoncello reminded me of a sunnier and warmer destination.

"Is that so? Where would you go?"

"The southern U.S. Florida or Texas. Someplace not far from the Gulf of Mexico. I'd love to be near beaches."

"Ahh, beaches. Yes, I can see you being happy with your bare feet in the sand."

Philipo brushed his shoulder against mine as he scooted closer on the sofa. I turned and his eyes locked onto mine. I sat up straighter and he got the hint and left a sliver of separation between us.

"After working a few years in Canada, then I'll see about taking a nursing job in the States."

"Will your children join you?" He asked a reasonable question. I didn't have a solid answer.

"That would be up to them, I suppose. I doubt I would move to the U.S. permanently. I'm a Canadian girl, you know!"

"Do you like your student nursing placement?"

"Brookhaven is challenging, and I am continuously learning. I'm glad to finally have the chance to work hands-on with patients." I was truly happy to be putting my nursing skills to good use.

"I've been watching you over these past three years, and I have no doubt that you will be a fantastic nurse, Julie." Philipo leaned to pour another refill as my phone rang. I jumped up from the sofa and answered the call.

Moments later, Philipo shrugged into his heavy leather winter coat and kissed both of my cheeks as he departed into the night. That had been Brookhaven on the phone. They were short-staffed and I accepted their plea to come in and cover the night shift. I placed the ornate limoncello bottle in the fridge, emptied my glass down the sink, and grabbed my nursing tote and keys. I scribbled a note to the kids—wait for gift opening until after my shift—and left it on the dining table.

I packed a Tupperware container with leftover turkey and potatoes and shoved it into my tote.

In the hospital locker room, I changed into my scrubs and then showed up on Brookhaven's oncology floor. The unit I worked on was surgical oncology, where they specialized in a lot of head and neck cancers. I had never been in such an intense placement before. The way this hospital ran was one-on-one RNs, meaning one RN would punch out at the end of his or her shift just as the oncoming RN punched in. There was no overlap. No discussions. Only a limited number of handovers of patient profiles. I had to quickly read up and brief myself on patient charts and any updates on care. I had assisted nurses on complex cases but had never been one-on-one all by myself with patient care. These patients had pretty complicated surgeries.

When I arrived for my shift, I was met by the charge nurse who barely acknowledged my existence. She sat at the nurse's station and leaned far back in a desk chair with her nose deep into a *People* magazine. She, I, and one other RN were working for this night shift. The doctors had tried to send as many patients home for the holiday as possible.

"I guess it's just you and I welcoming in Christmas morning," I said with a bit of holiday cheer.

She only groaned and didn't look up from the magazine. I could tell this was going to be a rough night.

One of the patients assigned to me had cancer of the tongue, so part of her tongue, jaw, and cheek had been surgically removed. She was missing a section of her lower jaw because the surgeon had cut a portion of her jaw and cheek in order to remove a tumor. It was my duty to inspect her wound and check the bandages. This patient had a tracheotomy and was under sedation. Carefully, I lifted the bandages and viewed the wound and the skin flap the surgeon had created. I couldn't let the patient's horrifying disfigurement, tubes, or monitors shake my concentration. At Brookhaven, there were no support staff such as PSWs (Personal Support Workers) or CNAs (Certified Nursing Assistants) to help with any hygienic or personal care of patients. I did all the personal care for my patients, if there wasn't a family member available to teach or assist. Post-OR, I would give the patient a bedbath and remove all dried blood from surgery. I remembered Doris's words every day when I worked a shift: "Think of your patient as your friend or mother." I made sure to give every one of my patients the highest respect.

My student nursing placement at Brookhaven was a great lesson in time management. I could be assigned anywhere between four to five patients during any given shift. Honestly, it was overwhelming and at times it was gut-wrenching, but I had to push all those emotions aside and focus on meeting my patients' needs for care and making them comfortable despite the rough condition they were in. Because of multiple IVs, trachs, and Foley catheters, the patients couldn't get up, move around, or even speak. I, alone, had the responsibility to physically turn them in their beds every two hours to prevent bed sores.

Over the course of that shift, I repeatedly walked past the nurse's station on my way to patients' rooms. The charge nurse didn't move a muscle the entire night. I was running rampant. It was the first time I had to care for all of the patients on my own. I missed one patient's call button because I was attending to other patients. I was completely exhausted, frustrated, and angered by the lack of concern from this nurse. She not only denied me any support, but she ignored our patients as well. What had I done to provoke this type of bullying? She obviously didn't want to work on a holiday, but still, we had patients who needed care, and she couldn't care less. When the morning charge nurse arrived a little ahead of my shift ending, she was baffled by the number of missed call lights. The nurse at the desk motioned to me and I glared back at her. I took the charge nurse aside and informed her that the night charge nurse refused to lift a finger. I left my shift with a feeling of discouragement and horrendous doubt. I certainly did not sign up for this.

CHAPTER 5

"Our greatest weakness lies in giving up. The most certain way to succeed is always to try just one more time."

– THOMAS A. EDISON

It was the middle of April 2004 when I came home after my shift at the insurance company and checked my mailbox. I ripped open an envelope and discovered the amazing news that I had officially passed the NCLEX exam! I was so relieved. In a couple more weeks, I would receive my nursing degree. I was so thankful that I didn't have to go to school any longer. No more studying! I could get on with my life and see what's out there for me.

Amber, Philipo, and I got together to celebrate. Amber, who was unwed and without any kids, had the tightest focus on studying and had the highest marks out of the three of us. She did so well and was a great help to me. I was so grateful for my friendship and connection with Amber and Philipo. Along with the nursing coursework, we also did a lot of lab work together where we learned how to do certain procedures and practiced on each other. I was going to miss the fun we shared in our study group. I don't think I could have passed nursing school without them.

The day of the NCLEX exam, I bummed a cigarette off of a student because I was so stressed out. I had stopped smoking after I had my kids, but leading up to the NCLEX exam, I needed a hit of nicotine.

Leading up to graduation, I gained hands-on training in various placements—long-term care facilities, nursing homes, and at Brookhaven Hospital.

I kicked off my shoes and waited for Amber and Philipo to arrive. I sat on my sofa and poured three glasses of wine. Philipo had a gleaming smile when I met him at the door. He proudly presented his NCLEX exam letter. When Amber came, the three of us posed for a selfie on Philipo's cellphone with wine glasses raised. Philipo informed us that he had accepted a position at a hospital in Regina[2] and would be leaving in two days. Amber accepted a position with a major teaching hospital in Toronto. They were genuinely excited about their new opportunities. I kept my fingers crossed for a full-time position at Brookhaven. Later that evening, Anne, Willy, and Natalie (who had also passed her NCLEX) stopped over with a celebratory cake. My entire apartment overflowed with joy! It was such a great feeling to know my kids were truly happy for me and what I had accomplished.

Just when I was about to open another bottle of wine, the phone rang, and I answered. It was the charge nurse at Brookhaven; they were short-staffed again. I gave another round of hugs, grabbed my work tote, and headed into the hospital.

As I came on for my shift, I was greeted by Betty, the Director of Oncology. I shared the good news with Betty that I had passed the NCLEX. She took me aside and we stepped into a small conference room. Betty was in her early 60s, gray hair in a sharp bob, and she always had her readers on a chain around her neck. All the RNs on the floor looked up to her for leadership, but she was also a nice and welcoming woman that I would consider a friend. Betty had been a Brookhaven employee for over 20 years.

"Congratulations on passing the NCLEX. That's a huge feat!"

"Thank you, Betty." I smiled.

"I wanted you to be the first to know that there's a full-time RN opening in oncology. You should apply, and I can provide a recommendation."

"Oh, that sounds terrific! I would appreciate your recommendation." I was thrilled by this news.

---

[2] Regina is pronounced "Re-gyna."

"Speak to human resources, and tell them I told you about the opening." Betty patted my shoulder. She rose from the conference table, and I did the same.

"This means a lot to me," I said, my voice quivering a bit.

"You mean a lot to the oncology unit, Julie. We'd be honored to have you as a permanent member of the team."

Betty left the conference room and went about her business. I stood frozen for a moment. This personal invitation to join the nursing staff was the perfect ending to this long-awaited journey. During my evening break, I checked out the human resources job posting board and submitted my application for the oncology vacancy. I made sure to write in Betty as my referral.

My relationship with Betty began after that incident when the night nurse sat and read her magazine. The charge nurse, to whom I reported the incident, passed it up the chain of command to Betty. Betty was very fair, and she talked to me about the incident. She asked me why I hadn't completed all the patient calls on my shift, and I explained that it was because I didn't get any help from that begrudged nurse. Betty was very good at keeping everything on track on the floor. She was a really good RN and had decades of experience in head and neck cancers. She was the kind of RN who was really good at attending to patients and providing excellent one-on-one care to patients.

She gave her staff additional vacation credits when she recognized post-traumatic stress. Probably, because she'd experienced PTSD herself. She granted time off for her nurses even if they didn't have the time built up in their PTO bank. She was great at being an advocate for the oncology RNs. She worked with them for higher job satisfaction. Betty understood that to have a good RN, management had to make it a place where RNs wanted to work, and retaining her best RNs was key. Betty and I connected on another level because when I told her that I had a bachelor's degree in history, she confessed that she had a bachelor's degree in a different field before pursuing nursing. She worked for a while, then entered nursing school to get her nursing degree. She and I were similar that way. There was a mutual respect we shared for our backgrounds and work history. I considered it an honor that she asked me, personally, to join her team of RNs.

As I walked through the hospital entrance at the start of my shift, I felt the surge of epinephrine (also known as the hormone adrenaline). This adrenaline-induced physiological response feeds a "fight or flight" reaction. My mental and physical awareness was heightened to help me deal with the workload of multiple patients with co-morbidities. This response also prepared me to work as quickly and efficiently as possible to meet my patients' needs in a timely fashion. Whether I dealt with medication administrations via IVs, topical, or oral. Focusing on treatments for wound care. Requesting and obtaining orders as needed from doctors, getting consents for ORs, collaborating with doctors and to advocate for my patients' needs.

Shortly after I started my shift, Marianna, an RN on my floor, came up to me. She was just a little younger than me and we had become friends during my time as a student nurse. Marianna was a pro with internal cancers like pancreatic and stomach cancers. She was thorough, and by shadowing her I furthered my learning and skills. Marianna helped to elevate my courage when it came to procedures, like Foley catheters and IV insertions. She was there when I was assigned my first Foley catheter. The patient was a woman, and I remember thinking, *Oh God, let me get this right the first time.* As a woman, I know how uncomfortable this must have been. Marianna watched me do it; she supervised and saw the urine as it appeared in the bag.

"There's urine, so you've got it in the right place." Marianna shot me a thumbs-up. A-ha! Victory! "Hey, can you come assist me with a patient?" she asked.

"Yeah, sure." I nodded.

I followed Marianna as we went into a patient's room. The male patient was severely overweight and had some kind of abdominal surgery to remove cancer. He had a huge belly with an incision all the way from his breastbone down to his pubic bone. The incision was stitched up with huge staples. The patient was asleep and still recovering from the surgery's sedation.

"I need your help. I want to show you something."

She lifted the blanket and showed me what was going on. Overnight, the patient's incision had dehisced (split open). Literally, his guts were spilling out of his abdomen. Marianna had called the doctor and notified him that this patient needed to go straight back to surgery. While waiting for the surgeon to arrive, we immediately prepared saline-soaked compresses and placed them over the split incision. It was a pretty gruesome sight, but I needed to be there to help Marianna avoid a real crisis with this patient.

Brookhaven was a teaching hospital, so there were always several resident doctors floating around on the floor. They heard about this patient and came to see this split incision. They had never seen anything like it! Neither had I! I had not even imagined anything like it. This patient's belly was like a scene from a sci-fi movie. I felt so sorry for the poor patient with his guts protruding.

"Wow, look at this," was the comment shared among the residents.

Finally, the surgeon and doctor arrived, and the patient returned to surgery. Marianna and I assumed he was okay, but he never came back to our floor.

Brookhaven usually scheduled me for least two 12-hour shifts, two days in a row, and hopefully I was assigned the same patients for those two days. I formed a relationship with these patients. As a RN, from the moment a patient enters the hospital, our process was to reach the goal of discharging patients home and for them to be happy and healthy. It was the nursing process using assessment, diagnosis, and outcomes planning to reach goals, implementation, and evaluation toward discharge. The cycle worked well for the administration to free up hospital beds for other incoming sicker patients. I got to know my patients and they got to know me, and in some cases, they would open up and confide in me. They trusted me with information about their health and personal situations. I always had to keep the "therapeutic boundary" in mind.

When I came on shift, I had to prepare myself mentally as I may not find the same patients as before. They might have been transferred to another unit, discharged, or in the worst cases, died. A lot of times, I never knew their final outcome. In that brief amount of time I spent with patients, it was a difficult challenge not to get personally attached to them.

Nursing was such a delicate, and at times intimate, profession because I cared for people in their most vulnerable state. They were clothed only in a hospital gown and had serious illnesses that needed my undivided attention. Inevitably, I ended up caring for not only their physical but emotional wounds as well. I had to deal with the disappointment of not knowing if any one of my patients had progressed or declined or was back to health at home.

A couple weeks later and after several interviews, I was offered the full-time position as a registered nurse in the oncology unit. I was ecstatic! For the first time in my life, I held the title of registered nurse. The first person I told was my sister.

"Jenny! I got the job! I'm an RN in oncology at Brookhaven. I just accepted the job!"

"Oh! That's fantastic, Julie! I'm so proud of you." Her voice glimmered over the phone.

"I'll pay you back for the loan in no time."

"There's no rush. You did Mom proud." And with that, both Jenny and I were tearful.

"Thanks, Jenny. I love you."

"Love you too, Jul. Now get out there and show 'em what you've got."

Our mother had died of colon cancer when I was 26 and in my se trimester with Willy. Losing my mom, while struggling with a faile riage and two little ones under the age of five, almost put me in a do spiral. Jenny, at the fragile age of 21, was also shaken by the dea mother.

My father and I had been estranged since I turned 19 and lef was a verbally abusive alcoholic. I was the only one in the ho challenged him and his mean ways. My mother was complace that generation where women didn't have options. They bec mothers and stayed trapped in loveless marriages. Through had unending and loving support for my sister and me. Sh out in the world, follow our dreams, and achieve our goals.

Accompanying my mom to her chemotherapy treatments, I was the positive one, with the eternal optimism that this medicine would help bring my mom back. She withstood the treatments and even tried experimental methods, but it didn't stop the cancer's progression. Having this life-changing experience with my mother gave me a higher sense of empathy towards patients with cancer and their families. It seemed so fitting, almost fate, that I was to become an oncology nurse.

Before I began my very first shift at Brookhaven as an RN, I had to make one stop. My car pulled into the parking lot at the insurance company. I was met by Gabriella, who gave me an enormous bear hug.

"I'm so proud of you. I knew you'd do it!"

"I appreciate all the support you gave me, Gabby. I'm so sorry that my cases will probably end up on your desk."

"Job security, eh!"

abriella giggled and I had to giggle too. I was really going to miss work-
h her and that infectious laugh of hers. Of course, this celebration
ew the attention of Mrs. Murphy. She immediately marched over.
k to work," Mrs. Murphy barked.
o my work tote and presented Mrs. Murphy with my nurs-
-da! I'm an RN, and I've accepted a full-time position at
I said confidently.
Murphy to stand there stunned and possibly rip the
to shred it into pieces. Instead, she latched onto
ed. Her eyes moistened.
ievement indeed!"
l and had been rooting for me all these
rief pause and shared in the congratu-
with boxes of Tim Horton's donuts

e office, I was more than ready
nd I experienced in insurance had a

lot of carry-over. The cases, paperwork, forms, and calls never ceased. The ongoing follow-up on cases and claimants was always churning. Whatever paperwork you left the night before would be there on your desk when you arrived at work the next morning. There was no room for fluctuation or a higher learning curve, whereas nursing offered the ability to work eight or 12 hours, and at the end of your shift, the next RN took over and cared for your patients. I could leave my shift at Brookhaven knowing that someone else was there to pick up where I left off. I knew patients were in good hands. I wouldn't have any worry that my patients were left unattended.

Unlike my insurance cases, I always had the worry that cases remained on my desk. No one else took up any slack. These cases were assigned to me and me alone. I'd never have that sinking feeling in nursing. In insurance, there was no "hand-off"—it was always me who had to complete everything from start to finish. I never felt like I could catch my breath. Because as soon as I closed or resolved a claim, there were at least 20 other outstanding claims that required my attention.

The main thing I liked about my insurance job was helping claimants who were truly injured and needed the justice and accommodations they deserved. But unfortunately, those people only made up about 25% of the cases; the other 75% were the cons.

Working as an RN at Brookhaven brought a huge change in job satisfaction. I had the satisfaction of seeing my patients get better versus dealing with people who were trying to con the insurance company out of money for false claims of injury. My Brookhaven patients had real wounds that needed my attention. I didn't have to rely on surveillance to give me proof that they were injured, like I did at my insurance job. These patients had serious issues like cancer or other diagnoses that required surgery. It was much more cause and effect. In insurance, I was always trying to prove the effect or find the actual cause of the effect. I spent a lot of my time disproving claims of a false effect.

One of my last cases involved a woman who claimed she would never walk again after getting hit by a grocery cart in a parking lot. In Brookhaven,

I had a patient who had a portion of her jaw and tongue removed due to cancer. She didn't have to prove to me that she'd never get to eat a steak again. I could witness this for myself. That's the kind of satisfaction I yearned for by entering the nursing field. I wanted to help people with the recovery process, not just be a step in their recovery.

CHAPTER 6

"Nursing would be a dream job if not for the doctors."
– Gerhard Kocher

Over two years have passed since I began my RN position in oncology at Brookhaven. I was on a learning curve, doing everything for the first time—remembering and recalling my training, my notes, my studying, my education, and following all the protocols. There was so much that filled my mind when I stepped onto the floor as a new RN. As an RN in her 40s, it may have been just a bit more challenging to recall all these things and act on them correctly and in the right order and manner. But practice makes perfect, and I managed very well. I was embedded in a team atmosphere and relied on my circle of RN friends. There was Marianna, who had become my confidant. She and I had so much in common with her being a divorcee and having two grown kids. Then there was Alise, who started around the same time as me. She was in her early 30s, not tied down by a spouse or kids.

I was thankful that Willy and Anne had become pretty self-sufficient adults. Both of my kids were in steady and happy relationships with a significant other. I was happy for them. Because I was lowest on the totem pole in the oncology unit, I worked alternating shifts. My work schedule was either 0700 to 1900 (days) or 1900 to 0700 (nights). Two weeks on 12-hour day shifts then switched to two weeks on 12-hour night shifts. This back-and-forth of days to nights messed royally with my Circadian rhythm. On the weeks when I worked nights, I planned to do chores and social visits. But by the time I awoke at 1500, it didn't leave much time for me to visit my kids, grocery shop, or cook meals. Plus, the charge nurse called me regularly for extra shifts, even four-hour shifts. Because I was short on cash, I would take the extra shift. It also great for me to hone in on my new skills. As chaotic as this routine was on my body and sleeping habits, I stuck with it because I loved the work and caring for my patients.

After the past two years, I had earned a reputation for my skills. Alise came to me recently and pleaded for me to do a Foley catheter insertion on a difficult patient. She and the other RNs hadn't any luck and this female patient was ready to strangle the next nurse that approached her. I went into the patient's room. She was a woman about my age, already in a great deal of pain and discomfort due to her cancer surgery. I chatted with the patient for a few minutes and asked about her pain level. She said it was a seven out of 10 (10 being the highest and unbearable). Due to her elevated pain, she was medicated. After 30 minutes, I was able to insert the catheter without any problems.

Betty had noticed my increased skill set on the oncology floor. I was commended for my nursing skills with a Certificate of Appreciation on my two-year anniversary. I was also asked by Betty if I would like to have student nurses shadow me and I happily accepted. I considered it to be an honor and duty to serve as a preceptor to incoming student nurses. Marianna and I each took a student nurse under our wing. Betty also approached me about a new opportunity. She had been heavily advocating with the hospital's administration for a specialized oncology center. It had been years in development, and the center was scheduled to finally open in the coming weeks. Betty needed RNs with oncology patient experience to staff the center. I was so elated to take on this new role. Betty also selected Alise to come on board with me at the center.

Just before the center opened, Betty scheduled a briefing with the center's RNs in the conference room. We were introduced to an RN who had transferred from the operating room (OR) to the oncology center. Her name was Farrah. She was a gorgeous young woman of Iranian descent who was in her late 20s. During our lunch break, Farrah told us about her journey from Tehran to Ottawa. A man she'd known since childhood had been matchmade by their mothers to wed her. She felt like she was marrying a stranger, and she hadn't seen him in years. Farrah was defiant of the traditions of her culture and thrived in her life in Canada. Farrah wasn't sure if she wanted to marry him or not. The government denied this man a visa to leave Iran, and he ended up in a jail cell in Tehran.

Her mother called in a frantic state saying that the man's parents sold off a piece of their estate to bribe the government to release their son. He still didn't have the proper paperwork to leave Iran, so he escaped to Turkey. Farrah was going to pay the rest of his expenses to get him out of Turkey so he could arrive safely in Ottawa. Canada was a country that motivated people to come to start a new life and find their happily ever after. She figured she could shelter the man and find out if they were truly compatible. The empathy Farrah had as an RN definitely came into play in this situation. It turned out that they were a good match. They married and now have one son.

When I worked at the oncology center, I would have a number of patients assigned to me. I became a stronger advocate and a better RN. I got to know my patients as they came in on a regular basis for their chemotherapy, radiation treatments, and management of chemo side effects. I was almost more of a nurse case manager than an RN. Betty handpicked her RNs. She found nurses who could benefit from a transfer to the oncology center. There was far less stress at the center than working on the inpatient floors. I gained much higher job satisfaction by working regular day hours too. Betty had a good eye for what could be a good fit for an RN to keep engaged and stimulated on the job. Betty had six nurses total for the center, and we were all oncology certified. It was great to know that if I was absent, there was another RN who knew how to assist my patient's needs. I really liked and appreciated Betty. She was the one person in my career that I knew truly had my back. Betty was always approachable and easy to talk to.

My job was stressful, but the excellent training I received made it easy. Dealing with administering chemotherapy had its own set of challenges. In one instance, I had a male patient who had come in for his first round of chemo. His wife was there to accompany him. After I had checked his vitals. I found his pulse elevated due to his anxiety about the impending treatment. This patient had been to the clinic prior to his treatment to have a PICC line inserted into his upper right arm. His anxiety was a normal emotional response to having his first chemo. Before I started the infusion, a second RN and I verified the patient's arm band and confirmed his identity and the correct med from his chart. The chemo he was having was going to be infused at a rapid rate over 15 minutes, referred to as a bolus. After the patient had his premeds, it was time to begin the treatment. It was customary for me to check in frequently with my patients. When I came to make my rounds, I found this male patient with an even higher level of anxiousness and confusion. He was trying to get out of bed. His wife was concerned.

"He's confused," his wife told me. The man's eyes were large and glazed over.

To the patient, I asked, "Can you tell me where you are?" He nodded his head yes. He calmed as I patted his hand and went on to check my next patient.

Upon my return, the patient's condition had severely escalated. He was on the verge of hyperventilating and was extremely fidgety. His wife was troubled by her husband's reaction to the chemotherapy. I applied an oxygen nasal cannula at a rate of 2 liters per minute to the patient, and it helped to calm him, but only slightly. It was within my scope of practice to place oxygen (02). A doctor's order wasn't needed. I had heard that RNs in the U.S. had to get orders for oxygen because it was chargeable.

I knew if I hadn't acted quickly, the patient would be in crisis. As it was, this patient was experiencing a negative side effect from the chemotherapy. He became so agitated so fast that he was reaching to yank out the IV. I had to call Alise for assistance. I reviewed the patient's chart and there was no order for Ativan, my drug of choice for anxiety. Before I called the doctor,

I stopped the chemo infusion due to the patient's state of confusion. I also needed an order to flush the PICC line with saline. I called the doc for an order of Ativan to help with the patient's confusion and combativeness.

The physician who answered the call was Dr. K. He was fairly new to the oncology center, and his inexperience came to light. No order was given, and he refused my request and thought I was being overly dramatic when I described the patient's condition. With my third attempt to convince Dr. K (and by this time he and I were extremely annoyed with each other), he finally approved the order.

"If it will make you feel better," he said in a condescending tone.

With the order in the chart, I then had to dash to the med drawers in the locked pharmaceutical room. There were rows and rows of skinny drawers pre-filled with packets of medication. I found the correct drawer and scurried back to the patient to administer a dosage of Ativan. After a few moments, the patient relaxed. I removed the oxygen and told the patient that his regular oncologist would need to see him the next morning. I charted the adverse reaction from the chemo in the patient's chart. I also offered the man's wife a cup of tea to calm her nerves.

During my time at Brookhaven, I had several discussions with doctors concerning my patients' care. It was so disheartening and aggravating when the doctors and surgeons didn't treat the concerns of nurses seriously. As RNs, we were the ones on the front lines with the patients; we had taken the time needed to get to know them and what was required for adequate care. I would present the patient's signs and symptoms and what action I felt was necessary. Usually, the doctors agreed and would give me the order I needed. If they wouldn't give an order, they would educate me on their decision.

It was the middle of winter when Alise and I were on our way to a dinner reservation when I noticed a billboard promoting a job fair in Ottawa recruiting RNs for jobs in the U.S.

"Wait! Did you see that billboard?" asked Alise.

"RN jobs in the U.S.?" I had only glanced at it, keeping my eyes on the road.

"Yeah! I took down the information." Alise jotted notes on a piece of paper. "I'll look it up on the web after dinner tonight."

Alise and I enjoyed treating ourselves to a fun dinner out occasionally. Being the only single RNs at the oncology center, we ended up being each other's "plus one" at special events. We both had a love for wine and warmer places. She had only traveled outside of Ontario once with her parents to visit British Columbia. She decided to get a passport on her 30th birthday, and she was itching to cross the border into the U.S.

"What if we got nursing jobs in Miami?! Wouldn't that be fabulous!" Alise downed a glass of chardonnay.

"Florida would be ideal. So many beaches to choose from. I've heard the beaches on the Gulf side are silky-feeling and white as sugar, and there's dolphins that swim in the warmer waters." I sipped my glass of chardonnay.

Alise casually flirted with our waiter when he dropped off a basket of fresh warm bread. She shared with me that she was in the middle of a "dry spell" with no action between the sheets in over three months. Three months! I think it had been over four years since I had a man in my bed. But three months for Alise spelled disaster.

"Do you think American men have a better grasp on what they want from women than Canadian men?"

"Maybe. There's one way to find out." We exchanged wild grins and waved for the waiter to refill our glasses.

The following Thursday, Alise and I took a vacation day and went to check out the job fair at the convention center. There were many booths representing hospitals from several regions of the United States. Alise and I, dressed in suit blazers and skirts, had supplied ourselves with updated printed resumes and made the rounds. I stopped and chatted with recruiters from hospitals in California, Florida, and Texas. One recruiter interviewed me right on the spot. She represented a hospital called Pablo Day General Hospital, located in San Antonio. My resume impressed her, and she considered my education, variety of experience, and level of maturity to be just what she was looking for.

"So, Julie, tell me about a time when you advocated for one of your patients?"

I told the recruiter about the experience I had with the male patient who needed oxygen and antianxiety meds because of a harsh reaction to the chemotherapy. Her eyes grew wide, and she leaned forward in her chair, engaged in the story I told about not giving up until I got the order from Dr. K. She was sold! She gave me a flyer about the hospital, made calls to the HR department, and scheduled me for an on-site interview. And she would arrange an all-expenses paid trip to San Antonio, Texas. I could hardly believe my luck!

"Are you serious?" Alise was floored. "Which hospital is this for?"

"Pablo Day General. Want me to introduce you to the recruiter?"

"For sure!"

I brought Alise to meet the hospital recruiter. Then I stepped away as Alise took her chance in the recruiter's hot seat. A few moments later, Alise had received the same offer as me. But she had to talk it over with her parents before making the decision to fly south. I had to discuss the same opportunity with Willy and Anne. This was going to be interesting to see how they'd respond.

Willy actually took the news pretty well. He was excited at the prospect that I might fly him down to visit me if I were to take the job in San Antonio. Anne, on the other hand, was miffed.

"What about the house?" she asked.

"I'll keep the house. I'll tell the tenants upstairs that they can keep renting and my apartment can stay as is. I'll keep paying the mortgage."

"Where would you live?" Anne inquired.

"I'd find a little unit to rent. I wouldn't be moving there for good. I only want to try this and see what the U.S. hospital system is like. I may hate it and come right back here."

"Texas? I thought you always wanted to be near water?" Willy had a point.

"San Antonio is just a couple hours' drive to the Gulf of Mexico. The temperature is around 60 degrees in the winter. Doesn't that sound nice?"

My kids couldn't hide the concern on their faces. I loved them dearly, even more when I could see that they'd miss me.

"I haven't been offered the job yet; this is just a second interview. Don't worry about me…about us." I tugged my kids into a tight group hug. The very idea of being separated from these two beings I gave birth to brought me a twinge of worry.

It was a bright sunny day in February when I landed in San Antonio. The temperature was a balmy 84 degrees. I arrived in the middle of a record-breaking heatwave. I took a taxi to my hotel and got situated. My itinerary for this trip included a round of interviews at the hospital and some local sightseeing. After I freshened up in my room, I decided to take a walk around the area. My hotel was located on the famous San Antonio Riverwalk. It was a beautiful and quaint area with shops and romantic restaurants along the banks of the San Antonio River. Lots of couples strolled arm-in-arm along the Riverwalk and I thought, maybe there's hope for me yet to find that special someone.

I found a seat on a bench along the Riverwalk and tilted my face to soak up the sun's rays. I could really get used to this.

I texted Anne to let her know that I arrived safely and was pleasantly surprised by the weather and local sites of the area. I didn't get an instant reply. She was probably busy and maybe was upset with me about mentioning the weather. It was a gloomy negative two degrees Celsius when I departed Ottawa that morning. After a delicious dinner at a Mexican restaurant, I returned to my hotel room and fell asleep to the local night sounds. It was a delight to sleep with the window cracked open in the middle of February.

The next morning, a taxi arrived and drove me to Pablo Day General Hospital. I met with Gladys, the director of oncology. She, along with two other members from HR and administration, interviewed me. After that, Gladys guided me to the oncology floor where I met the team: charge RN Diana and nurses Brooke, Madalena, Sam (a man), and Sarah (a travel RN). The entire team seemed welcoming. I didn't feel any kind of pandemonium, which was a good thing. They didn't give off any vibes that they were hiring me in desperation. After the team meet-and-greet, the rep from HR gave me a tour of the entire 250-bed facility. It was a much smaller hospital than I was used to at Brookhaven.

"We're proud to be the area's only community hospital," the HR rep told me on the tour.

"Our CEO, Paul Salito, has worked hard to solidify our place as a reputable center for care," Gladys added.

At the end of the tour, I was given a voucher for a free meal in the cafeteria. I went to check it out on my own as Gladys and the HR rep met in private. After a decent lunch comprised of a sirloin sandwich, salad, chips, and the freshest lemonade I had ever tasted, I returned to the HR office.

"Right this way, Julie," the rep said as he walked me into a small conference room. On the conference table was a colorful and branded folder for Pablo Day General Hospital. I opened the folder to find an offer letter. The offer was for an RN position in oncology reporting to Gladys, 56 hours per pay period (18 hours less than at Brookhaven), with full benefits and at a salary that was $25,000 more a year than my current pay at Brookhaven. According to the offer, I was to start in two weeks. I was stunned. Completely and utterly stunned. Was this too good to be true?

"A full benefits package?" I asked as I indicated to the offer letter.

"That's correct," confirmed the HR rep. "We highly value our nursing staff at Pablo Day General."

"This offer is remarkable," I replied. "But there's no way I can start in two weeks. Could it be adjusted to one month?"

"I don't see that being a problem. I'll check with Gladys to be sure. Feel free to take your time and read over this information. I'll be in touch with a new start date."

I picked up the folder and left the conference room. As I wandered my way to the main entrance, I was greeted by smiling faces and hellos. Cordial. The employees at this hospital seemed genuinely happy to work there. I sat in the shade of a Sycamore tree on the outer edge of the circular drive leading up to the hospital. The warm breeze felt so good on my skin. Seagulls floated in the blue skies above. There was only one thing left that could seal this deal for me.

The next morning, I left my hotel early, rented a car at the airport, and drove the interstate south until I arrived in the coastal town of Corpus Christi. It wasn't as tropical as I had envisioned compared to the images of Miami in my mind. I parked the car and made my way down to the beach, kicked off my shoes, and felt the soft sand between my toes. I sighed as the tide rolled in and out and crept my way into the water. With my pants rolled up to my knees, I waded along the shore and squinted my eyes as I looked up at the bright sunny sky. As my feet sunk deeper and the waves rhythmically flicked at my legs, I blissfully concluded that Texas would become my new home.

CHAPTER 7

"I'm not telling you it's going to be easy.
I'm telling you it's going to be worth it."
— ART WILLIAMS

One week before I was to begin my new job at Pablo Day General Hospital, I said my goodbyes to my kids and my cat. It was sad but I tried to keep it upbeat. I wasn't leaving forever, and I'd only be a phone call or plane ride away. I was still on the North American continent, at least.

Before my departure, I went through a lengthy checklist with Anne and Willy on how to keep up maintenance on the house. Our tenant in the upstairs apartment was a solitary professor who paid her rent on time and kept things tidy. I didn't have any worries about extending her lease. Willy and Natalie would take over the basement apartment. Anne would be the surrogate mommy to my cat, Chance. She and her boyfriend had their own place, and she liked the neighborhood. Anne was also in charge of keeping me updated on the house and sharing news about her and Willy. I was going to miss my kids and my cat terribly. But I was also excited about this new role in the United States healthcare system. However, I wasn't looking forward to the solo 29h drive from Ottawa to San Antonio.[3] My Chevy was stuffed with household items and my personal belongings. I triple-checked everything

[3] In nursing terms "h" used to refer to "hour."

before I got behind the steering wheel. I had given Anne, Willy, and Natalie big enough hugs that I hoped lasted until I saw them again. With a map on my passenger seat, I scanned my path. First, I'd enter the U.S. at the border in Detroit, take I-75 South to Cincinnati, then veer west and travel on and find a hotel somewhere between Nashville and Memphis to spend the night. On day two, I'd drive the remainder of the trip to arrive in San Antonio. I turned the key, the engine fired, and I bid farewell—for now—to Ottawa and my life there within.

As I drove past the San Antonio city limits sign, I had the radio on, and Stevie Nicks's song "Stand Back" blasted from my car speakers. Are you ready San Antonio? I have arrived! My Chevy pulled up to a historic two-story house in the heart of town. I chose this place because it was within walking distance of stores, and I wanted to familiarize myself with my new surroundings. It was also a brisk two-mile walk to the hospital. The landlord, Ron, who also lived in the house, rented out three of the five bedrooms. The good news was rent was priced very reasonably at $750 per month. But the bad news was, I only had a bedroom for privacy and had to share a kitchen and living room with the other renters—and Ron. He was friendly at the start, but by week six, Ron's odd duck behaviors were revealed and he was getting too handsy for me. Plus, because I was the only female in the house, somehow I had been appointed the house cook. No, thank you! I needed to get out from under Ron fast.

"He sounds like a major creep!" Brooke said when I told her about my situation.

My co-worker, Brooke, was close to my age. She had frosted hair in a snazzy blunt cut and the fanciest manicures I had ever seen. She and I got along great. She had two grown daughters and had been married for over 25 years. She and her husband lived in a fairly elegant house on the outskirts of town. I had attended a couple of wine-tasting parties for the oncology team that she hosted at her home. There was something special about sipping chardonnay under the starry San Antonio sky.

"Greg and I have a pool house that just sits there vacant. Let me talk to him. I bet he'd be open to letting you rent it."

"Are you serious? That would really help me out. Thanks, Brooke."

My fellow nurses on the oncology unit quickly became my friends. There was Sam, a male nurse who looked like he had just stepped off the set of Baywatch and slipped into a snug fitting pair of scrubs. Then Madalena, a beautiful Latina with long black locks that she always had in a tight bun atop her head with a gleaming smile that could stop traffic. Madalena was bilingual, which helped greatly with our Spanish speaking patients. We had a travel RN, Sarah, who was sleek and strong and a workout buff. If she wasn't at work, she was in the gym. Our charge nurse, Diana, had many years of seniority at Pablo Day General Hospital and knew all of the ins and outs of the system. I was grateful for Diana's patience as she trained me on these new-to-me aspects of the job. Lastly, there was our oncology unit champion, Gladys. She reminded me a lot of Betty. I immediately knew Gladys was the type of director who had her RNs' backs. It was recently announced that Alise, my former co-worker at Brookhaven, would be joining our team next month. I couldn't wait for the reunion with my Canadian friend.

There were several differences I noticed between being an RN in Canada versus in the U.S. First, there was the charting system. At PD General, the patient's medical record information was electronic. There was a portable computer on wheels that the RNs called the "COW." This computer went with the RN as they travelled from room to room making patient rounds. The COW also had locking drawers where you could store your patient's meds. All charting was to be updated and entered in real time or before the end of your shift. That brings me to one major difference. The shift changes. In Canada, there was no overlap of RNs at a shift change. For example, an RN would punch out at 1900, and the incoming RN punched in at 1900.

In the U.S., there was a 30-minute overlap for shift change.

My shift was afternoons, 1500 to 2330, 8.5 hours. I started at 1500, and the day RN's shift was over at 1530. During the 30-minute overlap, I received reports from the day RN on my five patients I resumed care for. Additionally, the hospital union was successful in establishing ratios. Each RN was not to have more than five patients. Only four, if one patient was having chemo. I thought this briefing was a great use of communication for patient care. We covered everything: how the patients did during the day, any tests, scans, or labs, and family visits. This discussion saved so much time and provided a good insight of the patients. A feature that was definitely lacking in the Canadian health system.

When I worked at Brookhaven, it was only RNs and the charge nurse on the floor. At PD General, we had support. Additional support. The patient care team was comprised of RNs, a charge nurse, LVNs who were fantastic at starting IVs, and certified nursing assistants (CNAs). One in particular was Claudia. We had a lot of shifts together. She was a sweet, muscular, young Black woman who looked like she belonged to a boxing club. Whenever the RNs needed a second set of hands, Claudia jumped right in, plus she did the personal care duties that I was used to doing as an RN in Canada. All the patients' showers, hygienic, and ambulatory care were taken care of by Claudia. I thought I had died and gone to heaven! I could finally focus on all the patients' medical issues, and I could put my education to good use. I learned to follow all of these new and helpful protocols.

A few months later, I arrived for my shift on the unit and went about my business like a well-oiled machine. Having the support staff at PD General really helped me to be efficient in my work. I learned how to increase my time management between evaluating and caring for my patients and keeping their charts updated in the electronic records system. I was an RN who worked hard to complete my meds' distributions, treatments, consents for next-day surgeries, and entries into the COW that allowed me to leave on time. Plus, I fit in some of our health stream assignments. These were courses RNs had to take yearly to keep current. Completing these courses during my shift meant I wouldn't have to return on my days off to do them. I liked and needed my downtime.

A typical day at PD General would consist of patients recovering from post-op. Our floor was also general med/surg overflow. Recently, one of my patients was recovering from TB (tuberculosis). TB patients received IV antibiotics and had to be in isolation until they passed three negative tests. Results were confirmed by chest X-ray and blood tests. My TB patient had only two negative tests and was removed from isolation. I spoke to Diana, the charge RN, and requested the patient be put back into isolation. Diana spoke to the nursing director that day. The patient was put back into isolation.

As far as I was concerned the protocols had to be followed. I was especially adamant when it came to infectious diseases. It proved to be a challenging and learning experience. This included pronunciation of certain names, said one way in Canada and another way in the U.S. Brooke and I were reviewing a patient whose name was Regina. I pronounced it, "Rah-ji-nah." Brooke shot me an odd glance and said, "Re-gee-nah," was the patient's name. She had never heard of the Canadian pronunciation and thought it sounded too close to "vagina." We shared a good laugh. It was like "tomato, tamato" I guess.

Thanks to Brooke, I had escaped my rented room at Ron's and found comfort and coziness in her pool house. I was really beginning to get my footing and forming some roots in San Antonio. My afternoon scheduled shift was 1500 to 2330, and I loved it! This gave me a chance to ease into my day, go explore the area, and come into work feeling refreshed and ready. I also got to spend time with Brooke's miniature poodle, Calvin. He was an adorable pup, and playing with him helped to fill the void I felt not having Chance around.

Meanwhile, Alise had arrived in San Antonio accompanied by her parents. Since their only child was making the move to Texas, they sold their home in Kanata (a suburb of Ottawa) and found a house in Austin. After Alise settled into her apartment, she went hunting for a cowboy. She spent her nights trying to convince me into bumming around with her at honky-tonk bars. The line dancing was fun, but I wasn't ready for the dating scene. I didn't know how Alise survived the social life she was accustomed to. Anne threatened to put my profile up on a dating website called "Plenty of Fish." She kept telling me there were "tons" of eligible men my age in the San Antonio area. I insisted that she let me find love on my own. I wasn't like

Alise. I was in no hurry to snatch up a man. I preferred a good book, a glass of wine, and a decent night's sleep.

On the oncology floor, there were two male patients who had identical diagnoses of testicular cancer. One patient was a Latino in his late 30s, and the other was a white male in his 20s. Both cases were under the care of the same physician, Dr. B. He was a notable oncologist who had prescribed the exact same chemo treatment for both patients. Both men were recovering from their treatments. The younger white male had family members who visited him in the hospital, his mom and dad. The Latino male didn't speak English and had no visitors, and no one to support him. When I made my rounds and checked in on the Latino patient, he was lying in bed, despondent, and his eyes had a faraway look. I noticed his Foley catheter still had rose-colored urine. The white male, on the other hand, was wide awake. He greeted me as he sat on the edge of his bed. His mom sat happily beside him.

"Hi, Julie!" the young man said when I appeared in his room pushing the COW. "Dr. B says that I'll be going home today."

"Yes, that's true. Dr. B put in discharge orders. I need to do a final check of your vitals, then go over your discharge instructions with you and your mom."

"I'll be glad to finally get this removed!" The young man pointed to his Foley catheter, which led to a drainage bag of normal, light-coloured urine.

"Are you experiencing any pain?" I asked as I listened to his heart and lungs with my stethoscope. Next, I placed the blood pressure cuff around his bicep and took the reading.

"Just some minor aches and pains," the young man replied. "Nothing too crazy. The meds are helping."

"That's good." I updated the patient's record into the COW. "Stay put, and I'll be back to remove the catheter and bring your discharge papers and printouts of medication information."

The young man and his mother smiled at me. The news of getting discharged always brought a smile to patients and their families.

In the hallway, I waved over Madalena as I made my way back to the

Latino patient's room. She hurried over.

"What's up?"

"Can you come with me and translate?"

Madalena nodded as we both entered the Latino patient's room.

"Please ask him if he has any pain?" Madalena interpreted in Spanish to the patient. He only shook his head no.

I wasn't buying his story. A full cup of water was on his bedside cart, untouched. His pale lips were a visible sign that he was in pain, and the minimal amount of blood-tainted urine in his collection bag was a sign that he was dehydrated.

"Ask him if it hurts to drink or urinate," Madalena interpreted in Spanish, and the patient only locked fearful eyes with us. He had no other movement or response.

I lifted his gown and noticed his lower groin was swollen and red. It looked like his tumor was growing. I offered him an ice pack to help reduce the swelling and elevated his scrotum on a small, rolled towel. I asked if he wanted pain meds. He responded yes to both.

"Ask him if he has someone coming to take him home from the hospital," Madalena interpreted in Spanish.

The patient replied with a faint voice, "No."

I focused intently and gently on the patient's face. "Do you think you should go home today?" Madalena interpreted.

The patient repeated, "No."

I think I've always had a sixth sense about people, and it grew when I worked at the insurance company, but when I became a RN, this sense flourished and has helped me immensely. It made me a really good listener. I've been told I have the kind of face and demeanor where people want to tell me everything. As a nurse, I came across patients who didn't communicate or chose not to communicate every detail about their condition. I had to be able to ask the right questions in order to give them the comfort and care they needed.

With a cancer diagnosis, people don't necessarily know there's something wrong with their body. The diagnosis can come as a surprise to many people. Other patients are known for having iron-clad mouths. Ask them anything, and they reply with "fine" because they just wanted to go home. Whether they were in denial about the cancer or made peace with their condition, the job I needed to do was to address their respected wishes. Other patients, who are notorious for not communicating with nurses or doctors, are those who suffered from abuse, alcohol, drugs, or victims of domestic violence.

Having the patience to listen and gain my patient's trust, allowed me to ask the pointed and pertinent questions and seek the answers to give the patient the best care possible. All the interviews I had done as a senior benefits investigator gave me the experience to listen attentively and extract great details. As an RN, I used my interviewing skills in a manner to become a stronger and more dedicated advocate for patients.

I turned to Madalena. "I need to let Dr. B know that this patient cannot be discharged today."

In the best interest of my patient's health, I went against Dr. B's order to discharge his patient. Instead, I had a discussion with Diana. She advised me to document everything in the COW and phone Dr. B with this update. Dr. B didn't agree with my findings. He had been tracking both of these patients and thought both had responded well to the chemo treatments.

"But they both recovered differently," I explained. "The younger patient has been drinking, following orders, and has his family to support his recovery at home. The other patient doesn't understand the orders, and doesn't even speak English, so how can he? And he's in a greater amount of pain and discomfort, and his drainage bag has rose-colored urine that I believe constitutes another day in the hospital in order to give him an optimal recovery."

Eventually, Dr. B showed up and reassessed the Latino patient for himself. After his assessment, he updated his discharge order to occur on the following day. I got a reputation among my fellow nurses as being a real bulldog when it came to advocating for my patients. I hadn't come this far just to be a pushover. Just when things were looking up, I found that I had four missed calls from Anne. At the end of my shift, I called her back.

"Honey, slow down."

Anne was babbling a mile a minute and sniffling. Something was obviously wrong.

"It's Chance. Something's wrong. He hasn't eaten in days and he's so lethargic. The vet wants to keep him overnight for testing. You know how much he hates being at the vet."

"What do they think is happening?" I asked. My gut was wretched to hear my daughter so distraught on the line. Poor Chance.

"They aren't sure. Maybe his liver or his kidneys, or both!"

"Keep me posted and give Chance a kiss for me." As I ended the call with Anne, Madalena approached me.

"Is something the matter?" she asked.

"Oh, my cat is sick, very sick. My daughter is distressed because it's my cat and I'm not there to comfort him—or her."

"Come with me. We'll go pray for your precious cat at the Mission."

"It's been a long time since I went to church," I said, suddenly feeling ashamed.

"Lucky for you, God doesn't count your absence. He only counts attendance." Madalena's lips curled into her famous gleaming grin, and it soothed my nerves. We wrapped up our tasks and made sure the incoming evening shift had updated reports on our patients before we left the hospital.

I figured I had nothing to lose by spending a little time in church. In my car, I followed Madalena as she drove up to the Mission of Santa Lucia. There was an old Spanish church in the Mission with colorful woven tapestries and what seemed to be a thousand lit candles. Within its adobe walls, it was a place of sanctity and peace. Madalena and I slowly walked up the center aisle. She knelt before a statue of the Crucifixion of Jesus and made the sign of the cross. I stayed a few feet behind until she rose, and then I followed her to the Santa Maria shrine where she took a wooden stick and borrowed a flame from a candle.

"Here, take this and say a prayer for your gato," she said softly.

I took the flame and lit a tall red candle, and as it flickered to life, I sent up a prayer for Chance. *Please, God, be with him, and help Chance to be well.* Madalena took a seat in a pew, and I shimmied in beside her. She wrapped her rosary beads around her wrists and whispered her prayers in Spanish. I sat in meditation and a light beamed down from the ceiling and landed on me. There was a kind of serenity and warmth in this Mission; it was more than just a place for prayer and worship. It was a holy gathering place for reflection and acceptance. A heaviness on my heart and mind seemed to lift as my eyes found even more candles had been lit on the altar. Glowing flames of hope.

I discovered a card in the pew. On the card, the Serenity Prayer was printed, one side in English and the other side in Spanish. It read, "God, grant me the serenity to accept the things I cannot change, the courage to change the things I can, and the wisdom to know the difference." I clutched the card to my chest, sucked in a breath, and tucked it into my purse.

After Madalena completed her prayer session, we walked down the steps of the Mission. As I left, I felt an overwhelming whole-body sense of tranquility. Madalena stopped as an attractive man came up to us. They exchanged a brief and friendly conversation in Spanish.

"Oh, Julie. This is José. He's a friend from the Mission."

"Nice to meet you, Julie." José extended his hand to me. His English was perfect. American-born, I assumed. The way he said my name gave me goosebumps. Did he see me shiver?

"Likewise, José," was all I could say. I felt my phone vibrate from inside my work tote. "Excuse me a sec." I stepped aside, fished out the phone, and answered the call from Anne. "Hello?"

"Mom! You'll never believe this. The vet called, and Chance turned the corner. He's perking up! He pulled out his IV and is up walking around his crate. They say he can come home later tonight but has to go on a special diet. We have money for that, right?"

"Yes! That's great news, honey, such good news! Yes, give the vet my credit card, and I'll pay for whatever treatment and food Chance needs. Thank you for being there for Chance. Get some rest. I love you, sweetheart."

"Love you too, Mom. Bye."

I squeaked out a tear and gasped in joy as I put my phone away. I spun back to José as he spoke.

"Madalena says you're new to San Antonio. Maybe I could show you around sometime?"

I glanced down at José's hand to check; no wedding band. Hmm...If I had to guess, I'd say he was 40-something. What was it about this town? First, an amazing job, a Mission that answered prayers, and now José. Another offer I could not refuse.

CHAPTER 8

"The very first requirement in a hospital is that it should do the sick no harm."
– FLORENCE NIGHTINGALE

In the summer of 2008, the economic downturn in the United States hit Pablo Day General Hospital and impacted the hospital's budget and bottom line. Employees took the brunt of it. Only six months ago, CEO Paul Salito and his administration handed out free Thanksgiving turkeys to the entire staff. Now, the hospital administration scrambled to cut costs wherever possible, the "happy" vibe in the building diminished sharply due to layoffs and cut-backs.

The CEO and the administration considered selling PD General to a large conglomerate. We heard about this potential sale from the nurses' union. Many changes would take place if PD General became part of this national chain. Changes could involve lay-offs and concerns for patient safety. The call centers and switchboards for patient scheduling and triages could be outsourced and decreased funds for hospital security. All of these issues heightened concern for the RNs at PD General. The hospital administration had engaged in a campaign of disinformation and was retaliating against union leaders. Nurses and other medical specialists were leaving in droves. It was obvious that the hospital administration's moral compass had plummeted, and RNs prepared to leave if the sale was finalized.

To boost team morale, the oncology unit staff met at Brooke's house to celebrate Sam, who was about to be a new dad, with a baby shower, and a bon voyage party for the travel RN, Sarah. She would be leaving for a position at Baylor Medical Center once Sam returned from paternity leave. We all needed this break away from the hustle and hectic changes at the hospital.

A mandatory change came from an email sent by the CEO which announced all RNs would have to increase shift scheduling. Our union negotiated with the hospital for the money-saving changes. Previously, the administration cared about patients and staff. Nurses were required to work 10-12h shifts. For years at PD Gen, the RNs had only worked 8h shifts. Ninety percent of the RNs felt these changes would impact patient care and lead to RN burnout. Diana had to bump us all up to fill these extended shifts. We were exhausted, but we never lost our primary focus, which was to still deliver quality care for our patients as best we could.[4]

Then, the next round of pink slips happened, and our charge RN, Diana, received notification that she'd been let go. The administration removed staff from the highest salaries. Diana opted for early retirement since she had earned a pension with her longevity of service. During the economic boom, Diana actually picked up a real estate license and padded her income with condo sales. She told us that she looked forward to being her own boss. All of my co-workers had extraordinary talents that turned into side hustles of one kind or another. Madalena and her husband, Angel, ran a catering business out of their home. She served us amazing tamales and enchiladas at the baby shower/bon voyage party. Brooke bred toy poodles for pleasure and a little extra "fun money." Claudia, the CNA, had skills for creating floral bouquets. She assembled decorative bouquets for weddings. The bouquets she gave to Sam and Sarah were gorgeous!

---

[4] Similar situations are happening throughout Canada. The Ford Provincial Government of Ontario introduced Bill 124 in 2019, which again introduces cuts to healthcare. This was evident in the 2020 COVID-19 crisis. The RN and support staff shortage put the healthcare system into crisis. Due to the staffing shortage, RNs were limited in their capacity to properly and effectively do their jobs to keep patients safe and healthy.

Staff on the oncology floor shrank to Brooke, Alise, Sarah, and myself. Sam was on leave. Madalena's and Claudia's hours were reduced by 50%. Not having those extra-skilled hands made our jobs that much harder. Even though times were tough, I felt somewhat secure in my position. Earlier that year, Gladys invited me to serve on some hospital committees with her. I learned more about the circle of care, patient-physician relationships, and insurance billing. I already knew a great deal about insurance from my previous experience, but I appreciated this deeper knowledge about American insurance plans.

Canadian healthcare was free. However, Canadians paid higher taxes than Americans in order to pay for healthcare. In addition, the Ontario Health Insurance Plan, OHIP, was shrinking their coverages. Eye care, for instance, was being omitted from the care plan. In rural Canada, primary doctors were few and far between. Doctors went south to the U.S. for better pay. Many Canadian citizens in rural areas had to travel to small hospitals just to get their prescriptions filled.

The reduced staff and new shift expectations at PD General put stress and strain on me and my co-workers and inadvertently affected our ability to care for patients. One of my patients, Mrs. Q, had a terminal diagnosis of pancreatic cancer. She had been in and out of the hospital for the past year. She was back again on the oncology floor for pain control. She knew she was dying and signed a DNR (do not resuscitate) document. I knew she was dying, and it wasn't a peaceful death. She had increasing ebbs of excruciating pain. I had to contact the doctor repeatedly to request a telephone order (TO) to up her dosage of morphine. Mrs. Q also begged me to contact her daughter. She desperately wanted one final visit before she passed. In between tending to my other patients, I left voicemails with her daughter. No one called me back. I no longer had Diana around to go to with these kinds of problems. I had to resolve them on my own.

At PD General, medication wasn't stored in a locked closet. Medication was in an electronically locked cabinet called the Pyxis MedStation. When I was hired, my fingerprints were collected so the administration could enter them into the Pyxis. You had to be granted access, and the pharmacy conducted daily audits on the medication removed from the Pyxis. Not only did you have to use your fingerprint to open the Pyxis, but you also had to enter an electronic username and passcode. Then an RN entered the patient's name on the screen, and a selected medication drawer opened, which held precise dosages. For every med withdrawn, there had to be a matching order from the patient's designated physician/prescriber. I couldn't just go to the Pyxis and get more morphine for Mrs. Q.

During my nursing career in Canada, I heard of RNs wrongfully accessing and stealing narcotics. In America, they had a much better handle on the situation. In addition to all of the highly complicated points of entry into the Pyxis, there were also security cameras mounted all around and one above the locked machine. Anyone using the Pyxis understood they were being recorded.

I called the doctor and received a TO (telephone order) for 2.5 milligrams of immediate-release oral morphine. With the doctor's approved order, I went to the Pyxis and entered my passcode, and a drawer unlocked and opened. This drawer was crammed full of individual dosages of morphine pills. I removed the correct prescribed amount and tried to close the drawer. It took me a couple of attempts to shove it shut, but it finally locked.

As I walked back to Mrs. Q's room, I checked in with Brooke. "Any callbacks from the daughter?" Brooke sadly shook her head no.

I relayed the disappointing news to Mrs. Q, and she cried. It crushed my heart to watch this woman weep. She was in her early 70s and was being robbed of an opportunity to see her daughter one last time. I administered her medication, stroked her hand, and checked her vitals. It wouldn't be much longer. But I couldn't tell her that.

"Rest easy, okay? I'll be back to check on you in a bit," I said softly. I handed Mrs. Q a tissue to dab her tears. For as much as I didn't want to leave her, I had other patients who needed my attention.

On my next check-in with Mrs. Q, she had indeed passed away. It was protocol to place a butterfly sign on an expired patient's hospital room door.

This signified the patient had died and did not require checks during rounds. Maybe the butterfly conveyed the message that the patient had spread their wings and hopefully arrived in the hereafter. I skipped my lunch break in order to prepare Mrs. Q's body before a staff member from the morgue came to retrieve her.

Dealing with a corpse is a grim yet highly respected obligation. As an RN, she had been assigned to me for this shift, and I was responsible for Mrs. Q until she was no longer on my floor. I took a washcloth and ran it under water. I used it to delicately clean her face. Her body temperature was still warm to the touch. I removed the IV from her vein that had provided her hydration and detached the Foley catheter. Her pain had been so intense the day before that she couldn't rise from the bed and use the toilet. I cleansed her arms, hands, and feet, then tucked the hospital gown neatly around her body. The cancer had reduced her to a thin shell of a person. Just like it had done to my own mother. I stood at the foot of Mrs. Q's bed and took one last look at her. She was at peace. I sent up a silent prayer. *God, please keep a watch out for dear Mrs. Q.* I had done my duty and once again maintained my therapeutic boundary.

The next day when I arrived for my shift, Gladys immediately called me into her office. I could tell by the concerned expression on her face that something was seriously wrong. Plus, she closed the door once I took a seat.

"Julie, yesterday you accessed morphine from the Pyxis machine."

"Yes, that's correct. I had the doctor's telephone order for my patient, Mrs. Q."

"The problem is there are six pain pills missing from the locked drawer you used."

My jaw dropped open. "Are you accusing me of stealing pain pills? I didn't."

"The audit report shows that there are six pills missing. I'm going to have to suspend you while we do an internal investigation."

"What? You're sending me home? But we're so short-staffed!" My shock turned into disbelief.

"Those are the rules. We have to follow them." Gladys rose from her desk and escorted me out of her office.

"Wait! That drawer was stuffed full of pill packages. I had to shove it shut. Maybe the machine miscounted?"

"I'll look into it. For now, go home, Julie."

Brooke and the others stood at the nursing station. I was so humiliated and filled with anger that I marched past them without saying a word and left the oncology floor.

A few hours later, my fury had simmered, and I called José. We had met up a few times for coffee and a movie. I really liked spending time with him. He thought I was a "genuine article" because I came from Canada. The only things he knew about Canada were hockey and the Toronto Blue Jays.

José was a huge baseball fan, and he was also a talented baseball player. When he was in college in Arizona, he was highly sought-after for the minor leagues. He decided his calling was to coach up-and-coming baseball players in the community. He also loved his recent role as umpire for the local leagues, and he was a lead official for all sports except lacrosse and hockey. He had never skated on ice.

José picked me up, and we took a drive down to Corpus Cristi. He knew how much I loved being at the beach. He packed a picnic, and we sat on a beach blanket and watched the sunset. He impressed me with the food he had lovingly prepared, hearty chicken sandwiches and a yummy pasta salad. After the sun went down, we walked along the seaside, meandered into tourist shops and bought cutesy souvenirs. I picked out a tie-dyed "Corpus Cristi" T-shirt and he, of course, found a branded baseball hat. Being with José gave me a feeling of real relaxation which I hadn't felt in years with a man. I could just be myself. I didn't have to entertain him or try to be someone I wasn't. We enjoyed each other's company and had great conversations. It was easy for me to be in a relationship with José. And I needed ease at this time in my life. I shared with José my journey from insurance to nursing and about my kids and Chance and how much I missed them. We both were survivors of failed marriages and had innocent hesitations for a new romance.

That evening, when he dropped me off at the pool house, I leaned in and kissed him goodnight. It took José a bit off guard, as he was the perfect gentleman, having always asked for my consent before holding my hand. That old song played in my head ("It's Now or Never"), so I went for it. My fondness for José was blooming, and I wanted him to know it.

"Have faith, Julie," José reassured me when I confided in him about the missing medication incident.

"I'll do my best," I replied.

"You always do," he smiled. After one more kiss, José drove away, and I did a little happy dance into the pool house.

After three days of suspension, I received a call from Gladys to return to the hospital. I was back on the schedule. Gladys met me when I arrived on the oncology floor. We went into her office, and she closed the door.

"Julie, we appreciate your patience while we investigated the missing pain pills. I remembered what you said about the med drawer. Diana had a similar instance a couple of years back. She noticed meds had fallen out of the back of an overloaded drawer and landed in the bottom of the Pyxis. That's the exact same case here. The missing six pain pills were located once a technician made an inspection and removed the back of the Pyxis. They never made it back into the morphine drawer. Your employee status has been reinstated, and the incident has been resolved."

"What is the pharmacy going to do so this doesn't happen again?"

"The incident is on their radar. It's not up to me to say what or how pharmacy will make amends. There's a lot of pressure in several areas to make do with less staff. I don't think I have to explain that to you," Gladys said. She pursed her lips and turned her attention away from me and onto a stack of files on her desk.

While I was glad to be back to work and exonerated, I got the sinking feeling that this was only the tip of the iceberg. During the three days that I had been away, I could tell that the morale of my fellow RNs had taken a deep decline. One ray of sunshine was that Sam had returned early from his paternity leave. His bright smile tried to hide the obvious fatigue brought on by sleepless nights with a newborn. He was proudly showing Brooke photos on his phone of Baby Jack.

"He's so adorable!" Brooke squeaked. "When are you going to bring him in for a visit?"

"Be careful what you wish for! I might just drop him off on your doorstep one of these days," Sam retorted.

Brooke squeezed Sam's arm tight, "Hang in there, Daddy. They grow up in a blink of an eye."

"They sure do," I added. "Soak up every moment you can. Babies are such a blessing."

Sam and Brooke briefed me on the oncology patients I was assigned to. One was a regular patient of mine, Mr. J. He was a lung cancer patient with a port in his chest for the immunotherapy. He was taking a new med recently approved by the FDA. Overflow from the tiny infusion center at PD General—which only had five stations—meant the chemo patients came up to our unit. Mr. J was in the middle of rounds of immunotherapy, with a regiment of receiving prescribed treatments every three weeks for six treatments. He was a widower in his early 60s who had confided in me that he only agreed to do the treatments because of his granddaughter. He hoped the treatment would keep his cancer at bay so he could attend his granddaughter's high school graduation the following spring.

After I checked Mr. J's vitals, I noticed a few little red bumps on his lower arm. I checked his chart and didn't find any notations for a rash. I wondered if it was a new side effect from his immunotherapy treatment.

"Are those bumps itchy, giving you any discomfort?"

"Oh, I didn't even notice them. I sat outside for a smo—" Mr. J caught himself before he accidentally confessed that he'd gone back to smoking. I was careful not to judge. My face stayed calm and gentle. "Probably mosquito bites from being outdoors last night," he tried to explain.

"Okay then, I'll get your treatment started. Here's the call button. You know the drill. Just press it if you need me for anything." I donned my chemo garb which consisted of a yellow gown and thick latex gloves. I called Sam to review the immunotherapy med and rate of infusion with me. Chemo medication administration always required two RNs to verify. I started Mr. J's IV line, and the chemo began to drip. He'd be in my unit for the next five hours. His type of immunotherapy had to be administered in slowly timed intervals.

On our lunch break, Sam told me about one of his patients. He recognized her from a prior hospitalization. She was an amputee who had returned to PD General from a nursing home facility. He noticed that she had a red rash, and it raised some suspicion.

"Do you think it's bed sores?" I asked between bites of my lunch.

"No, it's on her arms and is creeping up her neck," Sam said. "It's not shingles either, no blisters, looks more like bites. I need to do some more research."

Sam and I finished our lunches and returned to our patients. A few hours later, Sam rushed up to me. He spoke in a hushed tone. "Hey, Julie. It's scabies!"

"What? The rash?"

"Yes! I looked it up. The red bumps on my patient match the images I found of scabies."

"You should tell Gladys," I suggested.

"I can't find Gladys. Maybe she's left for the day. I need to bring it to the attention of the infectious disease staff."

"Can't you find another director or supervisor first?"

"There's no time. The longer it takes for me to find a supervisor, the quicker this will spread. I need answers, and I can't risk bringing scabies home to my family! Cover my patients for me while I send an email."

"Okay, sure," I reassured Sam. He sped off to the nurse's station and sat behind a vacant computer. Brooke leaned over his shoulder as he typed up a formal notification email to the infectious disease (ID) staff. Sam told us that he copied in Gladys and the ID director.

I peeked in on Sam's patient, who he deemed had scabies. I kept a safe distance and was able to note that she was resting comfortably. My mind reeled.

If we did have to move her into isolation, who would watch over our patients while we transported her? It was a dilemma since we were so short-staffed.

At the completion of Mr. J's treatment, I put on a pair of latex gloves and rechecked his vitals. As I removed the blood pressure cuff, I took a closer look at the tiny red bumps speckled on his lower arm.

"Is everything okay?" Mr. J asked. Honestly, I didn't know what to say.

"Looks fine for now. How are you feeling?"

"Right as rain, I guess. Toxic rain, perhaps. Ha!" Mr. J always tried to make the best of his treatment visits.

"Give us a call if you notice that rash increases," I urged without prompting too much urgency. I didn't want to alarm him. It was my job to stay calm, cool, and collected.

I wasn't 100% sure Mr. J had scabies. Or even if Sam's patient had it. A scabies test would be required to make the diagnosis. As Brooke, Sam, and I were getting ready to finish our shifts, I saw that Sam was extremely frustrated.

"No one has responded to my emails! Not a single reply!"

"Did you send a text for a doctor's order for a scabies test?" I asked.

"That request has been rejected as well. The doc's downplaying it. No Order. I'll bring it to the administration's attention if I have to." Sam was livid. Brooke and I had no luck in soothing his concerns.

My phone vibrated, and I grabbed it out of my tote bag. José was calling. I decided to let it go to voicemail. I was too rattled by what was—or wasn't—happening with Sam's plea for action. What if Sam wasn't wrong about the scabies? Just like I was wrongly accused of stealing meds?

CHAPTER 9

"To do what nobody else will do, in a way that nobody else can do, in spite of all we go through, that is to be a nurse."
– RAWSI WILLIAMS

Two days later when I arrived for my shift, there was an unusual hush and buzz on the unit. This odd mixture of whispers accompanied by a flurry of activity from the staff had my curiosity on high alert. This time, it was Brooke who met me and took me aside.

"Sam's been fired," she whispered.

"Really? Why?"

"Nobody knows for sure. The best I can guess, it's from that email he sent to infectious disease. The next day, he sent another email to the heads of administration."

"About scabies?" My question came at her like a bullet. Brooke only nodded.

"Have they ordered any tests?"

"No, and if I were you, I wouldn't ask either. Unless you want to risk your job too."

This entire order of events caught me off-guard. The oncology RN pool lost another employee and Sarah (the travel RN) couldn't stay in Sam's place because she had already accepted a position at Baylor. Losing Sam was terrible—on all fronts. I knew it would impact my workload. How could they fire him for this? My trust and faith in PD General's administration plummeted.

"And there's also this..." Brooke handed me a printed email addressed to all nursing staff from Paul Salito, the CEO. My eyes scanned the printed sheet.

"Mandatory whistleblower training? This is ridiculous! First, they deny Sam's claim, and now we all have to take time away from our patients to learn how to be an appropriate whistleblower?!"

"Shhh! Keep your voice down," Brooke warned.

"What about Sam's patient, is she still here?" I asked.

Brooke pointed to a patient room at the end of the hallway. I recognized the neon orange ISOLATION warning on the patient's door.

"So, she's in isolation... because she has scabies?"

"All we know is that she's an isolation case. There's nothing in her chart about scabies."

"Are we supposed to ignore that? This is ludicrous!"

"Concentrate on your patients, Julie. I'll meet up with you for the whistleblower training this afternoon."

Amazingly, last night after my shift, I watched a TV show called *Whistleblower*. They featured a hospital in southern California called Pacific Hospital. Two whistleblowers, a doctor, and an insurance adjuster became suspicious of a high number of spinal surgeries. The hospital performed so many surgeries unnecessarily. With such a high number of patients, they were running out of hardware. The investigation found the hardware was being fraudulently manufactured with substandard material. Many spinal patients were left in such pain due to the substandard screws and bolts. Most patients didn't need the operations they were convinced to have. It was a mess of lawsuits.[5]

Before Brooke glided off, she handed me updates on my oncology patients. I was assigned two female patients who both had identical procedures of

[5] Fast forward to a whistleblower case that happened in Toronto during the 2020 COVID-19 outbreak. Dr. Robert Fallis was let go of his position as medical director of critical care at William Osler Health System for speaking out against the Ontario government's delayed response to COVID-19. The Ford government even stated to the hospital administration that they would withhold funding to the hospital if Dr. Fallis didn't stop his criticism.

colon resectioning after cancerous tumors had been removed. Both of these patients coincidentally had the same first name, Cathy; their last names started with "M"; and their rooms were beside each other. Both women had discharge orders for today. Gladys had previously printed out the discharge orders and placed them on the COW. I skimmed the documents and entered the first patient's room.

"Hello, good news. Looks like you're going home today," I greeted the patient with a smile.

"She should've gone home yesterday!" grunted the patient's husband.

The patient's husband, Mr. M, had been a disgruntled ogre from the minute Mrs. M had arrived on the unit. He had multitudes of opinions about the care that was given to his wife. He barked orders at us like an armchair quarterback. Mrs. M, on the other hand, was a meek and mild woman who rarely spoke. Mr. M made it very apparent that he was the one who ruled over his wife and was crowned the spokesperson for her care.

"The doctor requested your wife remain in the hospital after the surgery. Mrs. M needed more rest for recovery." I turned my attention to his wife. "How are you feeling today?"

Before the patient could answer, her husband droned on.

"She looks fine to me. Got her color back, and she can pee and poop on her own. How much longer until I bring the car around?"

"Let's go through the discharge information and doctor's orders first," I said with a smile. Keep it cordial and professional, I told myself.

I picked up the front page of Mrs. M's discharge pages and read aloud the instructions to the patient. She was receptive to my smile and listened attentively while her husband fidgeted with his car keys. He did his best to be a distraction.

"The pharmacist indicates that you can go back on your Lipitor medication tomorrow..."

"Lipitor?" Mrs. M squeaked.

"My wife's never been on Lipitor! What's going here? Which pharmacist is saying that?"

I quickly glanced up to the heading of the discharge papers. I slowly read the patient's name printed at the top.

"Oh, my goodness. Pardon me. I got you mixed up with another patient. Her name is also Cathy."

"Wait just a darn minute! Are you giving us another patient's information?"

"It was a mix-up. I have the correct papers here," I said as I held up the correct discharge instructions. "Let's start over…"

"You admitted that you breached patient confidentiality. That's a violation of patient privacy. I want to speak to your manager!" Mr. M stood up out of his chair, ready to start a rampage.

I could feel my hands get clammy and perspiration leaked from my pores.

"Please, let's go over the correct discharge instructions so you both can return to the comfort of your own home."

After Mr. M gave out a guttural growl, he returned to the chair and sat glumly. I completed the details from the discharge report. I noted one last set of vitals from Mrs. M and moved on to my other patient, Cathy, in the room next door.

Being an RN required that I maintain total focus on my duties. I couldn't let my mind wander into the what-ifs. That is, until I walked past Sarah. I immediately noticed that she had tiny red bumps on her forearm. On my lunch break, I stepped outside the hospital and called Sam.

"Is it true they fired you because you blew the whistle on scabies?"

"Yeah, it sucks! I'm going to get a lawyer and file for wrongful dismissal. I'm also going to call the local newspaper. The public needs to know that Paul Salito and PD General turned a blind eye to it. They are endangering patients and staff!"

"Everyone's on eggshells here. They're downplaying it, keeping it hush-hush about the patient in isolation. Nothing indicating scabies."

"Watch yourself, Julie. You might get it next."

I understood Sam's motivation to talk to the media. I also thought that was a risky move that could backfire. There was an insightful magnet on our breakroom fridge that read:

"Nurses are a unique kind. They have an insatiable need to care for others, which is both their greatest strength and a fatal flaw."

– Dr. Jean Watson

Sam, like many RNs, had a fiery, hardcore Type A personality. RNs tended to be Type A, having traits such as being outspoken, determined, and forward-thinking. Being Type A is not learned, it is innate. These were key behaviors that contributed to being a shining advocate for patients. However, I had learned from experience that taking a step back to see the big picture was also an important part of being an advocate. Taking everything into account and reviewing the facts was a skill in which I excelled. I decided it was time to go on my own fact-finding mission.

CHAPTER 10

"Don't mess with me, I get paid to stab people with sharp objects."
– UNKNOWN

Alise and I sat at a cute little table in a quaint Tex-Mex restaurant on the San Antonio Riverwalk. Work on the oncology unit had been relentless, and it was rare for us both to enjoy the same day off the schedule. Alise still hadn't hooked a decent, good-looking cowboy to settle down with. She was enthralled that I had met José and wanted me to dish out all the details.

"He's really sweet and sincere, and we enjoy being together. But unfortunately, I've had to keep him at a safe distance."

"Why is that?"

I leaned in closer to Alise and whispered, "Well, because of the scabies."

"Huh! I thought that was just gossip," Alise replied as she sipped her margarita.

"Have you been following the protocols with the patient in isolation?"

"Of course!" she blurted. "I gown up, wear gloves, then afterwards ditch the PPE and gloves in the trash. Once I leave the patient's room and enter the connected anteroom, I wash and sanitize my hands."[6]

[6] This room refers to the anteroom, which is a small room attached to the isolation room. It has negative pressure with air flow to the outside. The PPE (personal protective equipment) gowns, gloves, and N95 masks are kept there. Once you leave the isolation room, you must discard the PPE in a special trash container, wash your hands in the sink, and then exit the anteroom. Most new hospitals don't have anterooms. Instead, they use Hepa filters in the isolation room and leave the PPE in

"Can't be too careful," I added.

"Scabies isn't in her chart," Alise whispered back. "Why would PD General conceal that?"

"I'm not sure. The whole situation is so peculiar."

"Poor Sam, he was only trying to do the right thing."

"Patient and public safety come first," I conferred. "Pretty shocking to know that Paul Salito is downplaying it, and so is the administration. It's got me wondering if we made the right decision by coming here to work."

Alise and I sat in silence and slowly savored our margaritas. The server who seated us approached—a young, attractive man with a bright white smile.

"I thought I recognized you!" he beamed.

I was flabbergasted. I wished I could place him. My mind went blank. He probably noticed my vacant stare.

"I was on the oncology unit. You're Julie, right? A nurse? You were there when I was discharged. My parents still rave about the great care you gave me."

The light bulb lit inside my memory bank! He was the testicular cancer patient! I didn't recognize him because he looked so incredibly healthy. He had a full head of wavy brown hair, a muscular physique, and an amazing skin tone. He was a walking, talking oncology success story. I reached out my hand and he shook it with vigor.

"Hello! So good to see you!" I exclaimed.

"Sorry to interrupt your dinner. I just had to come over and give you my thanks." He released my hand and walked away.

"Wow! Can you believe that?"

"I think you just got your answer. Patients like him are the reason we came to San Antonio," Alise remarked as we both raised our margaritas and tapped them in a toast.

The next day on the oncology unit, in addition to my regular inpatients, I

---

the hospital hallway. However, because of the lack of anterooms, an airborne virus as virulent as COVID-19 could spread rapidly.

was assigned two patients who needed outpatient immunotherapy infusions. Once again, the staff on the unit was stretched beyond our limits and the stress in the air was palatable. A knot in my stomach was forming as I knew this would be a challenging 12 hours.

One of my patients was Mr. J, back for his third lung cancer treatment. As I prepared to take his vitals, I couldn't help but stare at the red inflamed rash which was now visible on both of his arms. I grabbed a pair of latex gloves and quickly put them on. The tiny red bumps had spread and had inched closer to the port in his chest. I could no longer ignore it.

"Those red bumps, do they itch?"

"Like I'm on fire. I'm trying my darnedest not to scratch."

I decided to place the blood pressure cuff over his shirt sleeve to avoid aggravating the rash and I made a mental note to remove that cuff from the room after his visit. Mr. J winced as the blood pressure cuff inflated. His face displayed a great deal of pain.

"Have you been anywhere recently?"

"No. Just my home and here. I'm too old and tired to go galivanting around."

"Not even the grocery store?" I asked.

"Nope. My son brings my groceries...Come to think of it, he called this morning saying he's got this same nasty rash. Wonder what caused it?"

SCABIES! My blood began to boil through my veins. I wanted to scream from the top of my lungs, YOU HAVE SCABIES! And his son had it, too. That knot in my stomach hardened like a massive heavy stone. I knew this epidemic could no longer be ignored. I had to act.

"I think you should call your primary doctor. Tell them about this rash and get it checked out sooner than later. I can help you make the call if you'd like. Tell your son to get his rash checked out, too."

If Mr. J's case of scabies went untreated, the rash could keep spreading over his body and create horrible havoc on his health. Severe cases of scabies could lead to detrimental infections and even death. There's no way I would overlook my patient—even if PD General wanted me to. I was Mr. J's nurse, his concerns were my concerns, no matter what. I became an RN because I wanted to heal people.

I was committed to putting the welfare of my patients above all else, even if it meant jeopardizing my job.

Pablo Day General Hospital's administration was constantly trying to save money. They refused to make the RNs aware of the scabies outbreak and refused to provide any screening for scabies. Management did not take steps to prevent the spread of scabies among patients and staff. This wasn't the first time where actions—or reactions—by management stunned me.

At one point after the 2008 economic crash, there were rumors that management might close the oncology floor. They had the attitude that they could extrapolate these cancer patients to another hospital. The administration fixated only on the financial bottom line. This denial of the scabies outbreak by the hospital's administration upset me. How could they stand by and risk the health of hospital patients and employees?

While my frustration mounted, one of my chemotherapy patients was experiencing an adverse reaction. My patient, Ms. A, was undergoing treatment for colon cancer. Her doctor had prescribed an increased dose, because her recent CT scan showed the cancer was more aggressive than originally perceived. Ms. A had vomited and was struggling to breathe. I placed on 2LNC of oxygen (via nasal cannulas) and administered Zofran, an anti-nausea medication. As I tried to calm Ms. A, she convulsed and slipped into a full seizure. I halted the chemo drip and dialed 222 to initiate a "rapid response," which queued the rapid response team.

Ms. A was in crisis. The rapid response team quickly arrived and provided lifesaving measures to Ms. A. I disconnected her from the chemotherapy as she rested and regained consciousness. An hour later, Dr. S gave a TO (telephone order) to admit Ms. A for monitoring and further observation. Amidst all of the managed chaos of the rapid response team, I noticed one of the team members had tiny red bumps on his neck. That was the tell-tale sign that scabies had spread to other areas of the hospital.

On my dinner break, I decided to investigate the situation. I navigated my way to two different floors and split my break time into separate breakrooms. I sat quietly, ate my food, and struck up small talk with RNs in the general surgery and cardiology units. I counted visual signs of scabies on at least six different RNs. One commonality I also noticed was apparent fatigue. Twelve-hour shifts and high patient populations were a combination headed for disaster.

After my shift, I took a long hot shower. I agreed to a visit with José. But only if we sat outside the pool house and in separate chairs. I was exhausted and he could sense something was wrong. I broke my silence and told him about the scabies outbreak. José showed me a recent Austin newspaper. Buried within its pages was an article about Sam and his whistleblower case with PD General. It was a small article, easily missed, but it bore Sam's name and set the alarm of scabies at PD General. I called Sam immediately.

"Sam, I just read the article."

"I tried to get in the San Antonio newspaper, but none of the reporters would return my calls."

"That's strange; it's happening right here."

"I kind of regret going public. I've gotten calls threatening to pull my RN license. My lawyer is getting nowhere with the wrongful dismissal suit against PD General. The hospital says they are a government entity and can't be sued. They're also claiming I violated HIPPA!"

"I'm so sorry, Sam. But I appreciate you sounding the alarm."

"Take care, Julie. Bye." There was sincere sorrow in Sam's voice.

José 's eyes locked onto me. His gentle gaze let me know he cared. Cared deeply. I desperately wanted to hug him, but I stopped myself. I needed to keep him safe. José suggested that I leave PD General and find another RN position elsewhere. It would have been an easy way to avoid the situation, but it wasn't in my DNA to take the easy way out.

The next day, I woke up to discover red bumps on my upper arms. Despite all my best efforts, I had caught scabies. In less than an hour, I was to appear for my shift at the hospital. It was too late to take a sick day, I persuaded myself to report for duty mostly because I knew there were no other RNs available to cover my shift.

When I arrived at the hospital, Gladys asked me to accompany her to a conference room. I was surprised to find members of the administration and HR in the room. I immediately bristled at their stern faces as I took a seat. Gladys sat with the others on the opposite side of the oversized mahogany table.

"Julie, several instances have come to our attention. Mr. M, a patient's family member, spoke at length with me about a discharge incident where you violated HIPPA," stated Gladys.

"It was an honest mistake. I apologized to Mr. M," I replied.

"Mr. M has also contacted Paul Salito and threatened legal action."

"That's crazy!" I could feel my cheeks redden.

"As outrageous as it may seem, we have no choice but to enforce disciplinary action. Yesterday's incident with your patient and the rapid response team. The doctor feels that you were inattentive towards his patient and could have prevented the crisis from escalating."

"But she was having an adverse reaction… How was I—"

All of their judgmental eyes locked onto me. I found myself in the very same hot seat as my insurance claimants. I was guilty until proven innocent.

"Security cameras captured you wandering floors of this hospital during your shift. Again, being inattentive to your patients," the HR rep alleged.

"I was on my dinner break."

"That doesn't excuse you from distracting other employees. RNs on those floors confirmed that you had conversations with them," Gladys continued.

"And by that rash on your arm, you've knowingly come to work spreading a contagion." One administrator pointed at my exposed arm.

"Julie, your employment at PD General is hereby terminated effective immediately," the HR rep reprimanded.

"We have contacted the police, and they determined that there's probable cause to have you charged. You've been criminally negligent. You're being charged with criminal negligence causing bodily harm."

The conference doors opened, and two law enforcement officers entered and stood behind me. The officers hoisted me up out of my chair. In an instant, I was handcuffed and rushed through the hospital. I stiffened and felt numb, like an out-of-body experience. As I was whisked past my co-workers, I caught a glimpse of their astonished faces. My feet barely touched the ground as the officers linked their arms through mine and hauled me away.

CHAPTER 11

"Never doubt that a small group of thoughtful, committed people can change the world. Indeed, it is the only thing that ever has."

– MARGARET MEAD

I was in hell. An eight-by-five-foot interview room at the Bexar County Jail where I was trapped, recorded, and interrogated by the Chief of Police, Grant McDonald, and Cameron Blain, the Assistant District Attorney. The ADA was a sharp-dressed man, younger than me, and from his loosened tie and collar, I figured he was as overworked as me. It was difficult to focus on his line of questioning. The scabies on my arm provoked a ferocious impulse to itch and I wanted to crawl out of my own skin.

"I need to be seen by a physician," I pleaded.

"What for?" Cameron snidely asked.

"This!" I shoved my red rash-covered arm six inches away from his face. "I'm pretty sure it's scabies. You don't want it spread all over this jail, do you?"

Cameron flinched. "What is scabies?"

Through gritted teeth, I answered, "Scabies are parasites that burrow under the skin. You don't know you're infected until the red raised bumps appear. The parasites leave microscopic feces that needs to be scraped off skin in order to be tested."

Cameron grimaced. "Is this what you were spreading around PD General Hospital?"

"That's their accusation. The truth is I was tracking down the scabies, which is still running rampant at the hospital. It didn't start with me."

"I want to know why someone like you, a nurse with a spotless track record, suddenly goes off the rails and becomes criminally negligent of causing bodily harm." Cameron had his pen poised in his grip, ready to document my confession on his bright yellow legal pad.

You're sheer out of luck today, pal, I thought. "I want a lawyer. And I want to make a phone call."

Cameron pursed his lips in frustration and stood up. He threw his pen down on the legal pad and crossed his arms. I was done playing nice.

A nurse came into the interview room and conducted the scabies test on me as Chief McDonald watched. I released a sigh of relief. When Cameron returned with a cellphone, beads of sweat formed on my forehead as panic washed over me. I had no idea who to contact for representation.

"Make it a quick," Cameron glared as he handed over the phone.

The more pressing issue was to inform my family. It was important that they heard directly from me that I had been arrested. Jenny answered the call.

"Jenny, it's me. Don't talk, just listen. I'm in the Bexar County Jail in San Antonio. The hospital had the police arrest me on criminal charges...I didn't do it...It's all part of a huge cover-up. Please don't cry, Jenny. I'm so sorry I can't tell Anne and Willy myself. You have to let them know. I'm innocent. I'm getting a lawyer. Tell the kids I love them so much, and I love you too. I have to go...Goodbye, Jenny."

Hours later, I slathered permethrin topical cream over my scabies rash. The remedy took a while to take effect. Slowly, the itching subsided and I felt terribly alone in my solitary quarantined jail cell. I wanted to crumble from the unbelievable and unsurmountable circumstances. I couldn't show weakness, and I refused to collapse under the strain of my misery. I was a victim of false imprisonment. I shuddered when I thought about the jail's intake process–inking my fingerprints, snapping my mugshot, assigning me an inmate identification number, and confiscating my personal clothes and belongings. I sat alone on the prison bunk and was forced to do some hard reevaluating of the decisions I had made in my life. Did I regret becoming an RN? Absolutely not. Had it all been worth it? It was. I had to suppress the tsunami of emotions that welled up inside me. I felt as if I could explode and implode all at once. Worry was like a shark with razor-sharp teeth. It waited patiently just below the surface, eager to devour me. The haunting torment came to an abrupt pause as a Chief McDonald came to unlock my cell.

"Come on, you have a visitor," he groaned.

The door to my cell opened and the officer ushered me back to the interview room. I was met by two serious yet friendly faces, one male and one female.

"Julie Findlay, I presume?" The man was first to speak. He was short and wide in stature, with dark hair and sideburns. His suit attire was quite a few paygrades below the assistant district attorney's.

"Yes, that's me."

"I'm Jason Kushner, your appointed lawyer, and this is Laurie Sanders."

"I'm a legal nurse consultant," Laurie said warmly. She was older than me, bronzed complexion in a fitted skirt and blazer with hair coiffed in a sleek chignon. These two definitely dressed the part of legal professionals.

"How did you know I was here?"

"We've been hired to be your defense team," replied Jason.

"Hired by who? My sister?"

"We are keeping that confidential for now. Let's just say it's someone who thinks you're a client worth defending."

Laurie motioned to my medicated rash. "Is the medication helping with the scabies?"

I nodded.

"There's a lot of questions I need to ask you," Jason asserted. "Before we gather your side of the story, we need to get you out on bail. You need to be healing at home, not in here."

"That would be great!" I was elated at the possibility of being sprung from jail.

"Of course, you'll need to surrender your passport. Can't have the judge worrying you're a flight risk," added Jason.

The thought of escaping back to Canada hadn't even crossed my mind—but it did now that he mentioned it.

"I can call a friend, and she can bring it in for me," I offered.

"Fine, good," said Jason. "Let's get started. We're already behind the eight ball since Cameron and PD General's legal team have stockpiled evidence against you."

"It's falsified evidence. I'm not guilty of anything except one minor mix-up with a patient's paperwork and taking my break on a different unit."

A deafening silence fell upon the cramped interview room. I was angry, confused, tired beyond reason, and frankly, wasn't in the mood to play 20 questions. The only thing rattling around in my brain was one burning question: who the heck hired these two?

My bail hearing was expedited, and I appeared before a judge with Jason and Laurie the next morning. By midafternoon, I was released on bond, which José provided by taking a second mortgage out on his modest home. I felt terrible that he had taken on such a huge financial burden.

"I believe in your innocence," was all José said to me. I owed this man my life and my freedom.

After a long hot shower and a six-hour nap at the pool house, I called Jenny and my kids. I talked Jenny out of flying down. It uplifted my soul to speak to Anne and Willy. They even got me to laugh when they told me about the shenanigans Chance was up to. My cat was protesting his litter box and leaving them "presents" in their slippers. When I was feeling more like myself again, Jason, Laurie, and José came to see me, and we continued building my defense case.

"Cameron Blain and PD General's legal team have presented us with a deal," Jason said as he handed me an envelope. I opened it and read the official document. My jaw dropped.

"This says if I plead guilty, they will ask for 24 months of supervised probation and revoke my nursing license indefinitely. I…I'm not guilty!" My hands shook as I tossed the letter at Jason.

"If you take this deal, it will keep you out of jail, Julie," Jason advised.

"What happens if I refuse the d-deal?" I asked with a quiver in my voice.

"The only chance of saving you from a prison sentence is to bring the case before a jury at trial," Laurie said softly.

"And a jury could convict you to five to seven years in prison," added Jason.

"I'll take my chances with a jury. Someone's got to believe I'm innocent." I breathed long and hard, trying to calm my shattered nerves. My watery eyes met José's comforting gaze, and my heart rate immediately lowered. All the shame and horror I kept inside melted away. José made me feel loved and secure.

"If a trial is what you want, then we need real answers," Jason responded in a stern tone. "First, why didn't you go to your manager when you knew about the scabies?"

"I didn't know it was scabies for certain. They didn't order any tests," I replied.

"So, this was all speculation on your part?" Jason's questions came at me like rapid gunfire.

"The red bumps and rash were consistent with scabies and Sam said..."

"I don't care about Sam's case. I'm only concerned about your case, Julie. Stick to the facts."

"An email went to infectious disease and to the administration warning about the scabies patient. No one came to test, and the next thing I knew, the patient was put into isolation. There's nothing in her chart about a contagion, only that she's to be in isolation."

Laurie and Jason's eyebrows raised, and they shared a curious side glance.

"Someone from infectious disease had to have sent that isolation order," Laurie muttered.

"Yes, but they didn't tell the staff why. It was such a peculiar case. That's when I started to notice that RNs on our floor had red bumps. It was spreading. I had an admission for a frequent flyer patient. She returned for pain control. When discussing her patient history, she stated that when she was discharged from her last admission, she went home with scabies. She knew she got it from the PD General, and so did her family doc who made the diagnosis," I continued. "Additionally, there was a travel RN who thought she had mosquito bites. She left and started a new job in Michigan. The bites turned out to be scabies, and she accidentally started a spread at her new hospital."

"Did the other RNs suspect scabies?" Laurie inquired.

"There were mumblings, more like gossip. Then Sam was fired, and we all had to go to mandatory whistleblower training."

"How absurd!" Laurie blurted.

"I know! That's what I'm trying to tell you. PD General was on a witch hunt. They were more concerned with keeping staff quiet than keeping us—and patients—safe! If anyone on the floor spoke about the possibility of scabies, they were either dismissed or fired."

"Why did you decide to go speak to other RNs on the other floors?" Jason's eyes were filled with wonder.

"Because I had to see for myself if the scabies had spread to other areas of the hospital. And it had."

"Do you have any form of proof?" Jason asked.

"I have a couple of photos on my phone of RNs who showed me their red rashes. They were afraid to call in sick—like I was—for fear of losing their jobs. PD General had made so many cutbacks, everyone was worried they'd be the next to go."

"We can subpoena the email sent to infectious disease and HR records of staff reductions at PD General," Laurie suggested. She and Jason expressed a unified look of optimism.

"I'm starting to feel better about this trial option," Jason grinned.

"We will need testimonies from other RNs. Julie, can you give us a list of names and their contact information?" Laurie remarked.

"Here comes one." I smiled as Brooke appeared.

"Here's all the proof you need as to why Paul Salito and PD General's administration kept scabies under wraps. They couldn't—and wouldn't—allow scabies to destroy their stellar reputation." I slammed the newspaper down in front of Jason.

"Paul Salito and the high-priced legal team may think PD General is untouchable," Jason snickered. "If we follow the scent of money, that's where we'll find the stench."

"We could smell that dumpster fire from a mile away!" I chuckled.

Brooke joined in on the joke with a wicked cackle. "'Employer of choice,' not a chance!" she spouted.

Weeks turned into months, as Jason and Laurie did their own investigation and collected evidence in my defense. They interviewed my fellow co-workers and recorded their witness testimonies. They even contacted Mr. J, who was more than willing to share his story and the scabies that interrupted his cancer treatments. Everyone freely cooperated. I could breathe again. Jason and Laurie dug into HR information and found video recordings from security cameras at Pablo Day General. Unbeknownst to me, I was under constant surveillance. The administration built a campaign to entrap me. It was mind-boggling to Jason and Laurie as to why the staff was coerced into keeping Sam's whistleblowing a secret. The hospital's action of making everyone attend whistleblower training was their attempt to distract from the whistleblower's claims. PD General's administration wanted to make a negative example of the whistleblower. My legal team was building a case that defended me and put the blame squarely on the shoulders of Paul Salito and his administration. PD General created a wrongful situation more as a game of risk versus appropriate patient or employee care.

After that newspaper article came out, Paul Salito was hailed as a shining community leader. It infuriated me when Brooke or Alise gave me updates on his rise to power. There was an abundance of wealth, power, and influence in San Antonio, and now Paul Salito ranked among them. He had been invited to speak at the Chamber of Commerce, and he was asked to be the keynote speaker at the Texas Hospital Association's annual meeting. As for me, I had Jason and Laurie to thank for keeping my name and face out of the newspapers. So far, I had avoided harsh scrutiny from the public. Laurie, being an RN, understood my commitment to my career and how I would never jeopardize that by admitting guilt and becoming a felon.

Over the endless hours we spent preparing for the trial, Jason and Laurie knew it was preposterous that I had compromised patient safety and violated HIPAA. There was proof on my employee record that I had maintained my education on HIPAA confidentiality rules and Joint Commission Standards. In order to keep my RN license current, I was required to complete hospital Health Stream education courses yearly. One of those courses involved infection control. From my background in insurance, Jason and Laurie accepted why I had taken on my own covert scabies investigation. They knew I was a truth-seeker. The veil of ignorance by the hospital's administration was being lifted. Jason and Laurie discovered Paul Salito, along with his top managers at PD General and the hospital board, to be the underlying reason behind the cover-up, which was way bigger than just cutting costs—PD General's underlying excuse.

The day before the trial, my case hit the media. My family had arrived and José transported them from the airport to a hotel where I clutche them tight in a bear hug. The sight of my children made my heart soar. that same moment of happiness, I felt a pang of terror and concern. My and accusations were splashed all over local and state media channels. warned me that this media blitz was unavoidable. After Jason and Lau for the evening, it was just me, my kids, Jenny, and José.

"We know you're innocent, Mom," Willy whispered in my ear. want to release him from my hug.

"We wanted to be here for the trial," added Anne.

"Your support means more to me than you'll ever know," I couldn't control my emotions any longer. I held tight to my k as Jenny and José huddled in for the group hug. The physical family gave me the emotional boost I needed to get through situation.

CHAPTER 12

"Never give up on anybody. Miracles happen every day."
– H. JACKSON BROWN, JR.

The red clay monument of the Bexar County Courthouse looked more like a museum than a beacon of justice with its bronzed pioneer statues … founders and the triple-teared fountain. This monolith in the heart … Antonio embraced the history and grandeur of law.

…vas the fourth and final day of my trial. Cameron and the hos- …eam had spent the past three days compiling what they con- …n ironclad case against me. They contested my loyalty as an …erated wicked lies and negative fabrications of my employ- …al team, Jason and Laurie, had collected evidence of my …ords, which contained letters of praise from patients …ns the administration and management had given … and recoveries over the years. This volley of us …n me. I was depleted and ran solely on adrena-

…hill streaked across my body and gave …ame space that had been occupied by …ok my seat next to Laurie and Jason …cted and kept my eyes forward. …ameron Blain and the "darkside lawyers" of the PD General legal team seated at the prosecution table.

At dinner last night, Jenny took me aside. She was worried about me and rightfully so. "Julie, you've barely eaten anything this week. You need to keep your strength up."

"I don't have much of an appetite," I told her.

This morning, I noticed my gaunt and unrecognizable complexion, and the mirror never lies.

My kids sat two rows behind me alongside Jenny and José. Before I entered the courtroom, José squeezed my hand as his prayer beads slid down his wrist. I'd take all the prayers I could get! It was a packed audience. I recognized Sam and his wife, Peggy, seated near the back. A month ago, Sam had accepted a settlement with PD General on his wrongful dismissal case outside of the courts. As part of the terms of his settlement, he was not allowed to testify in my case. He and his family would soon relocate to Arizona.

Yesterday, as Alise sat outside the courtroom awaiting her call to the witness stand, she succumbed to the intimidation tactics by the PD General legal team. They threatened to revoke her nursing license and have her parents deported back to Canada if she testified. When Anne took a bathroom break, she saw Alise make a run for it as she fled out of the courthouse. Anne trailed Alise, but Alise escaped into a taxi. Anne quickly and discreetly alerted Jason and Laurie of Alise's departure. Jason had to request an emergency recess to lure Alise to return.

"I can't believe the dirty deeds of the PD General lawyers. These threats are clearly witness tampering!" Jason was peeved.

He gently yet firmly reminded Alise that she had been subpoenaed to appear in court. Laurie assured Alise that she would not lose her nursing license by testifying. As for her parents' risk of deportation, Jason said that the U.S. government had an immense backlog at the immigration office, and Alise shouldn't worry about it. Eventually, Alise gave an emotional testimony.

As much as Jason and Laurie wanted to hunt down Paul Salito and Pablo Day General Hospital, they were adamant about staying focused on my trial case. Their commitment and steadfastness impressed me and my family. They showed no signs of backing down. But their optimism couldn't dislodge the stone that formed in my throat as I watched an officer of the court corral the 12 jury members into their jury box. Jason reassured me that these jurors went through a rigorous selection process. They all either had been an inpatient or were employed by or had a loved one employed by a healthcare center. The faces of the 12 were plastered in my memory. I mustered every nerve and fiber in my body to remain professional. But with every breath I took, I knew my life was at stake. These jurors were my appointed "caregivers" as my life was now in their hands.

The court stenographer took his seat below the bench as a clerk stood and read from a document.

"All rise for the Honorable Judge Leonora Martinez presiding."

Everyone in the courtroom stood at attention as a petite, robed Latina with readers that dangled around her neck took her officiant seat behind the bench. The clerk continued, "These proceedings are a continuation of case number 88832106 Pablo Day General Hospital and the State of Texas versus Julie Findlay."

"Counselors, today is your last opportunity to call upon any further witnesses and to give your summations to the jury," Judge Leonora stated as she perched her readers onto her nose.

Since the start of my trial, Jason and Laurie tried to convince me against taking the witness stand. But I had to give my testimony. I was compelled to tell the jury my side of the story.

Last night, Jason and Laurie made a last-ditch effort to keep me off the stand.

"Are you ready to be grilled by Cameron? The PD General legal team has been paid to be ruthless. The cross-examination will be grueling and detrimental to any kind of future you may have, Julie."

"I'm as ready as I'm ever going to be!" I declared. "I need this chance to tell the truth."

"You already know that they don't care about the truth. And they don't care about you. They only care about winning this case and protecting the reputation of Paul Salito and his managerial directors at PD General Hospital. Laurie and I truly care about what happens to you."

"I appreciate that and everything you and Laurie have done to defend me." My stare bore deep into their solemn gazes. "It's time I defend myself."

"Whatever happens on the stand, don't let it rattle you. Stay vigilant, Julie," Laurie hailed.

"You can count on it!" I declared.

* * *

Jason rose to his feet and addressed the court. "I call Julie Findlay to the stand."

I stood and glanced down at the pink skirt and cardigan Jenny had helped me pick out for the trial. Laurie encouraged me to look as professional as possible. My blonde hair, which was normally flowy, was pinned back, and I clasped my hands together as I proceeded to the witness stand. After the formalities of being sworn in to "tell the truth and nothing but the truth, so help me, God," I took my seat in the witness chair.

Jason slowly approached and tilted his poise so that he faced me as well as the jurors. "Please state your name for the court?" Jason asked.

"Julie Anne Findlay."

"Thank you. Julie, according to the testimony of Police Chief McDonald, you were diagnosed with scabies. Is that correct?"

"Yes," I replied, leaning into the microphone.

"Can you please tell the court where you contracted scabies?"

"At Pablo Day General Hospital."

Cameron flew up from his chair. "OBJECTION! Your Honor, that's speculation."

"Sustained," Judge Leonora responded. Cameron resumed his seat with a smug sneer.

"I'll rephrase the question," uttered Jason. "Was there any other environment you were in, aside from your job and home, where you could have been exposed to scabies?"

"No, I was working a lot and didn't have time to go anywhere else besides home and the hospital."

"Do you live alone?"

"Yes."

"So, no one else shares your home with you?"

"Yes, that's correct."

"I see. So, if there wasn't anyone in your home with scabies," Jason spoke slowly, clearly, and with a hint of clever wit, "and unless those pesky microscopic mites banded together and somehow jumped into your car, biding their time to infect you…"

A few murmured snorts floated out of jurors as they tried hard to control their amused expressions.

"Then, it does seem plausible that you were infected with scabies from Pablo Day General Hospital, doesn't it?" Jason finished.

"Yes."

Cameron squirmed as Jason went on.

"Why, when you saw the first signs of scabies, did you decide to still go in for your shift at the hospital?"

"I didn't know for sure it was scabies. No one had been tested for scabies. I hadn't been tested."

"The Pablo Day General Hospital administration hadn't ordered staff to be tested for scabies?" Jason asked.

"No, not that I know of," I replied. "The PD General hospital administration had not ordered or offered scabies tests for staff or patients."

"Did you ask to be tested?"

"No," I admitted under my breath.

"Can you please repeat your answer?" the judge politely instructed me.

"No," I said loudly. "I did not."

"Why not?" Jason asked as he stepped closer and leaned one elbow on the witness stand. His forehead tilted in my direction.

"Because I was afraid I'd lose my job if I mentioned scabies."

"Are you referring to whistleblower retaliation?"

Cameron bolted up from his chair and made an angry gesture in Jason's direction. "OBJECTION! Your Honor, Pablo Day General Hospital is not the one on trial here!"

"Well, it should be!" retorted Jason.

Judge Leonora pounded her gavel with authoritative aggression. *BAM! BAM! BAM!* "Overruled. Counselors! I'm warning you! Mr. Blain, retake your seat. Mr. Kushner, continue and get to the point."

"Yes, Your Honor," answered Jason as he calmly stroked his lapel and his ego. "Now, where was I? Oh yes. Julie, please tell the court why you feared for your job?"

"The other RNs and I were not made aware of any scabies infections from the hospital administration. But one of my colleagues brought it to the attention of the infection control department. There was a patient who showed signs of scabies but was not placed into isolation. The next day, that colleague was fired, and the patient was put into isolation on my floor. But there was nothing in the patient's chart to indicate an infectious contagion. Days later, several RNs on my unit had red bumps on their skin, which were signs of scabies."

"But you didn't know for certain because the hospital didn't order any tests for scabies?"

"Yes, that's—I mean, no, they did not order any tests." My brain blurred. Jason rested one hand on the banister of the witness stand. He helped to ease my nerves.

"Which is it, Julie? Yes, the hospital administration did order scabies tests, or no, they did not?"

"No, there were no scabies tests ordered."

"How many staff members in the hospital would you say you saw with these red bumps?"

"At least 30."

"Were these staff members approached by management or sent home when they came to work with these red bumps?"

"No."

"Did you come to work that day, with the tiny red bumps on your arm, because you were just doing what your other colleagues were doing? Keeping your shift schedule?"

"Yes. We were short-staffed. If I didn't come in and work, there might not have been another RN to take my place."

"You've always looked out for your patients, haven't you, Julie? Keeping their health and well-being in the highest regard?

"Yes, always," I stated with conviction as I scanned the curious faces of the jury.

The corner of Jason's mouth curled into a slight smile. "No further questions."

"Would you like to cross-examine the witness, Mr. Blain?" Judge Leonora inquired.

Cameron exhaled long and slow. "Yes, Your Honor." He slid his chair back and marched toward me with a flare of arrogance. "Ms. Findlay. Isn't it true that anyone—whether they are a member of the public, a patient per se, or a staff member—can go to the PD General ER and report scabies symptoms and request to be tested?"

"Yes, I suppose so."

"Would that prove that the hospital administration wasn't preventing anyone from being tested for scabies?"

"But they should have been proactively testing staff when they knew about the scabies!"

"Your Honor, I motion for Ms. Findlay's comment to be stricken from the record," Cameron demanded.

"So moved," Judge Leonora nodded at the court reporter, who in turn nodded back at her.

"Just answer the question, Ms. Findlay. Did the Pablo Day General ER allow people to be tested for scabies?" Cameron repeated.

"Yes," I mumbled.

"Louder and into the microphone, please," ordered Cameron.

"Yes."

"Not only did the hospital allow for scabies tests, but there was also testimony from the infection disease RN that she sent a memorandum to staff about scabies precautions. You heard that testimony, did you not, Ms. Findlay?"

"She lied."

Cameron threw up his hands in frustration. "Your Honor! Make her answer the question!"

Jason shot up from his seat and slammed his hands down on the defense table. "OBJECTION! Stop badgering the witness!"

Judge Leonora raised her gavel. Her eyes grew wide behind her readers. *BAM! BAM! BAM!* "Order! Order in my court! This is your final warning, counselors. One more salacious outburst, and I'll see you both in my chambers!" *BAM!* Her white knuckles released the gavel as it came to rest.

Rustling could be heard from the court audience. My gaze landed on Anne's teary eyes. I had to shake my head to clear the terror and disappointment displayed on my daughter's face.

"Ms. Findlay, answer the question," Judge Leonora said, exasperated.

"Fine. I do not recall any such memorandum." I crossed my arms in defiance. I wasn't going down without a fight.

"Your legal representation has said that you went to those other floors in the hospital to speak to RNs and conduct your own investigation. Is that correct?"

"Yes."

"Investigating what, exactly?"

"Whether the scabies had spread onto other floors beyond the oncology unit, and it had." My voice was stern. I didn't respond directly to Cameron. I was aiming at the jurors.

"Did the other RNs tell you that?"

"They had the red bumps on their arms. I could see it for myself."

"But you just testified that you weren't completely sure whether those red bumps indicated scabies. Correct?"

The stone in my throat reemerged and garbled my words. "Yes, I suppose."

"By doing your own investigation, you weren't playing by the normal rules of employment, were you?"

"Their rules. PD General's rules. But being an RN means I always play by the ethical rule of upholding the best care possible for patients. As an RN, I was the first line of defense against any contagions, and I wanted patients and staff to be safe." My eyes pleaded with the jurors. I intended to pin any hope upon their consciences.

"Wouldn't you say that you were making up your own rules as you went along?" Cameron wickedly narrowed his eyes at me.

"OBJECTION!" Jason's face reddened, and I saw Laurie reach over to restrain his upward arm.

The stone in my throat turned into molten lava. I felt as if my entire insides were on fire, and I wanted to thrust my fist at Cameron. Instead, I pursed my lips and clutched my hands onto the witness chair.

Cameron spun on his heels and walked back to the prosecution table. "No further questions, Your Honor."

Judge Leonora pivoted to me. "You may be dismissed."

I stepped down out of the witness stand and shuffled past the jury to my seat at the defense table.

"The court will take a recess and reconvene in one hour for summations," the judge ordered as she tapped her gavel.

The clerk barked, "All rise!" Judge Leonora glared daggers at Jason and Cameron, then strutted into her chambers.

Encircled by my family and José on the lawn outside the courthouse, I teetered from dehydration. The San Antonio heat was stifling, and the humidity was almost suffocating. Laurie handed me a cold Gatorade and I rolled the icy bottle along the base of my neck. José cracked the bottle open for me. I gulped the cool drink.

"Maybe we should go back inside, for the AC?" Jenny suggested.

"No! I like my freedom out here. Hades heat and all!" That quip got a rise out of my family. My kids giggled. "I'm really missing Ottawa right about now!" I threw my arms tight around my kids as our laughter came to tears. They shielded me from the encroaching paparazzi. I heard fluttering camera shutters in the distance.

Soon after, we were back inside the courtroom. While I sat behind the defense table, Laurie rubbed my shoulder as Jason neatly stacked his sheets of notes. I twisted in my chair to give a smile to my precious family and José. To my surprise, Gladys was seated at the end of their row. I hadn't seen her since the day of my arrest. It was puzzling that she had decided to appear on the final day of my trial.

Cameron stood before the jury to present his closing argument. "Here are the facts, ladies and gentlemen of the jury. Julie Findlay was a registered nurse employed by the Pablo Day General Hospital. Within her employment record, there was a mishap with narcotics distribution, a reported violation of patient privacy and HIPAA regulations, and lastly, a covert investigation that involved her tapping into other floors of the hospitals, potentially committing further violations including negligence and criminal bodily harm. May I remind you, dear jurors, that my client, the Pablo Day General Hospital, is not the one on trial here. It is Julie Findlay who knowingly came to work with a highly contagious infection, and spread it to areas of the hospital, other than her usual floor, thereby endangering the health and wellbeing of patients and people in our community with bodily harm. She knew that her motives were negligent, and she needs to be held accountable for her actions. The prosecution rests."

Cameron gave a boastful nod to Judge Leonora, who only scowled back at him. Jason cleared his throat and waited for Cameron to sit. There was a blanket of silence over the entire courtroom. Jason's shoes scuffed along the wooden planked floor as he rose and took purposeful strides to center himself in front of the jury.

"The defendant, Julie Findlay, is the kind of nurse any hospital or medical center would be thrilled and honored to have as an employee. She's dedicated to her patients and upholds the highest standards of care. She's demonstrated that she pours 110% of herself into her work, and she's received an impressive collection of accolades during her years of service at Pablo Day General Hospital."

I watched the jurors' faces as they hung on Jason's every word.

"Then, everything changed after the economic crash. PD General imposed unrealistic expectations on its nursing staff, making it mandatory to work up to 12 hours per day sometimes, up to six days in a row. Julie was thrust into an environment of endless uncertainty as her team of RNs were reduced by 50%, yet the patient population continued to increase."

Jason demonstrated with his hands. One hand rose high as his opposing hand dived low.

"Take a moment to think about this, ladies and gentlemen of the jury. How can management expect fewer RNs to provide the same quality of compassionate care as patient loads increase?"

The visualization of Jason's arms spread wide vertically captivated the jurors along with the courtroom's audience.

"Now, you tell me if there's any logical way for these two means to meet in the middle. Let's add to the stress and strain of having an overextending workload and fearing for your job security by having a gag order put upon you by the hospital's CEO and administration. Imagine knowing there's no one you can go to for help. You're expected to stay on this hamster wheel of a healthcare system day in and day out. If you spoke out against it, you faced termination. They didn't uphold the whistleblower protections under the law; they denied protection of staff who voiced their concerns. Valid concerns. The ultimate betrayal of an employer who exists for the primary purpose of protecting the health, safety, and wellness of those they serve." Jason was steamrolling his argument with gusto.

"Pablo Day General Hospital is renowned in the community as a pillar of healthcare according to the front page of the San Antonio newspaper—an article that Mr. Paul Salito paid to be printed as part of his ploy to fully demonstrate the hospital's commitment to community health. We have provided evidence that all the while, he and his administration knew that scabies was running rampant in the hospital. If Mr. Salito and the administration were focused on upholding their commitment to patient welfare, they would have ordered and implemented scabies screenings and protocol. But they kept the contagion concealed. Ladies and gentlemen of the jury, we have presented sufficient evidence that the negligence was not on the part of the defendant—my client, Julie Findlay. On the contrary, Julie tried to do everything in her power to protect patients and co-workers from the contagion." Jason paced methodically from one end of the jury box to the other.

"Remember, your job as jurors is to put together *all* of the facts. If Julie was as deviant as the prosecution would like you to believe, what did Julie stand to gain by spreading scabies to patients and staff? Why would a highly acclaimed nurse risk her livelihood, career, self-respect, and public humiliation by doing her own investigation?" He paused and motioned in my direction.

"Julie was on an urgent mission for the truth. Yes, she was willing to risk her job, but it was for the greater good—the truth about scabies, which PD General kept concealed. She was trying to save lives as only a nurse can. Thanks to Julie and brave whistleblower employees like her, the scabies secret is out! And it is *wrong* for Julie to be punished for uncovering the truth." Jason's hand swung in the direction of the prosecution.

"It all boils down to the Pablo Day General Hospital's administration under the leadership of Paul Salito, who recklessly hid information on scabies, which in turn violated the protection of the hospital's patients and the health of the hospital's patients and staff." Jason leaned heavily over the railing of the jury box and spoke with sincerity.

"Think about if you or a loved one went into the hospital. Whose hand do you place your life into? Their hands! It's the administration that keej the hospital's doors open. The CEO and the administration are responsil for *everything* that happens within the walls of the hospital. And they arє blame when bad decisions happen. Not nurses like Julie. Find the defenc not guilty of criminal negligence causing bodily harm. Julie was abidir her oath to provide quality patient care. The only thing she's guilty of is doing the right thing. Thank you."

* * *

José and I were hand-in-hand on an early morning walk. There was normalcy in some exercise. The kids and Jenny were still asleep at the hotel. It had been two solid days since the jury had been sequestered. As the sun rose in the east, my cell phone rang. It was Jason. Judge Leonora's clerk summoned us to return to court.

Two hours later, the courtroom was filled once again with a packed audience, my defense team and I, along with Cameron Blain and the conniving PD General legal team.

Judge Leonora looked to the jury. "Will the jury foreperson please stand?"

The jury was comprised of sleep-deprived, flustered, and displeased faces. A woman in her 60s glanced at me and then stood.

"Is it true that you and fellow members of the jury have reached a verdict?" Judge Leonora asked the foreperson.

I felt Laurie reach beneath the table to squeeze my hand. I trembled.

The foreperson's voice quivered, "Yes, Your Honor."

"Thank you. You may be seated."

The judge is handed the jury's paper. Judge Leonora scanned the docu-
nts before her on the bench and then looked out over the courtroom. Her
landed squarely on me. Goosebumps rose up on my skin.

ie judge handed the note back to the bailiff, who returned it to the
okesperson. "Please proceed," said Judge Lenora.

pokesperson began, "In the case of Pablo Day General Hospital ver-
Findlay, on the count of criminal negligence causing bodily harm,
guilty."

nora states in a loud, clear voice, "NO ORDER to convict!" She
vel with a mighty *WHACK!* "You are free to go, Ms. Findlay.
journed."

Cheers erupted from my family. An audible gasp burst from my mouth.

"YES!" Jason was elated.

The tumultuous trial ended. As Jason and Laurie led me out of the courtroom, a hand reached out and stopped us. It was Gladys.

"I guess this is as good a time as any to tell you that I paid for your legal team," she said. "I knew you were innocent, Julie. I couldn't say anything because of the administration. I hope you can forgive me." I grasped Gladys's outstretched hand. Her support was the remedy that took my battered and bruised psyche from critical to stable condition. Jason and Laurie ushered me through a whirlwind of people to the steps of the courthouse. A reporter shoved her microphone at my face.

"Julie, you've been freed. Do you have anything to say?"

I swallowed hard, and that stone in my throat vanished. Never to return.

"When you're a nurse, every day you touch a life, and a life touches you. As a nurse, it's not just *who* I am; it's *what* I can do that counts!"

AFTERWORD

We are the CEOs of our own health board. In order to thrive, we must convince the government, private enterprise, and insurance companies to work in collaboration towards the goal of a united healthcare front.

Elizabeth McCormick is a Registered Nurse licensed in both Canada and the United States. In her debut novel, *No Order*, she draws on her nursing experience to craft a powerful story of resilience, transformation, and hope.